FERAL NATION

Convergence

ALSO BY SCOTT B. WILLIAMS

The Pulse
Refuge
Voyage After the Collapse
Landfall
Horizons
Enter the Darkness
The Darkness After
Into the River Lands
The Forge of Darkness
The Savage Darkness
Sailing the Apocalypse
On Island Time: Kayaking the Caribbean

ISBN: 9781687689832
Cover & interior design: Scott B. Williams
Editor: Michelle Cleveland

FERAL NATION
Convergence

Scott B. Williams
Feral Nation Series Book Six

Dedicated to Ruth Tripp, with gratitude to a great teacher

One

THE MOVEMENT THAT CAUGHT her eye was slow and deliberate, and Shauna Hartfield would have missed it completely if she hadn't been carefully scanning the banks of the creek below her as she sat motionless among the boulders of the rocky slope above. Hunting wasn't really a necessity yet, and she didn't plan to be here long enough for it to become one, but it was a good excuse to get out of the confinement of the cabin, and it gave her the feeling of doing *something*—anything other than waiting. She'd been out since shortly after daylight and had hiked a couple of miles down the heavily-wooded drainage below the cabin with one of Bob Barham's scoped deer rifles, a bolt-action Remington 30.06.

The outcrop from which she watched seemed like a good place to spot a mule deer or perhaps even an elk visiting the little swift-water stream, and at the very least, the view was nice and was far enough away from Jonathan and Vicky for her to get lost in her thoughts for a while. Shauna would take the shot if game presented itself, even though packing the meat back would be quite a chore and would require her to go back for one of the horses. Jonathan would be little help with his mobility still limited, and she and Vicky would have to do the bulk of the work. Still, fresh venison would be a welcome change in their diet and would enable them to conserve more of the considerable stash of supplies Bob had stored there at the cabin.

Shauna carefully raised the rifle and brought it up to her shoulder so that she could use the scope to identify whatever it was that she'd seen moving. It had been a long time since she'd hunted, but she remembered that even the subtlest of movements that might be mistaken for a bird or other small animal could sometimes indicate the presence of big game: perhaps in reality the flick of an ear or tail, or ripple of light on hide or antler... The magnification of the 3x9 variable scope would reveal the truth, but even before Shauna could bring the telescopic sight into line with what she'd seen, she saw something else take a step in the same area, and it definitely wasn't a deer or elk, because it appeared to walk on two legs!

Shauna felt her heart race as she eased the scope over to this new movement to get a better look and make sure she wasn't imagining things. If someone was really there, they weren't moving now, and she couldn't pick out the outline of a body. It was only when her crosshairs moved over the man's bearded face that she could be sure he was real. The rest of his body from his boonie hat down was covered in camouflaged clothing, and even the weapon he carried at ready, as if expecting an ambush, had a muted camo finish. When the man took another step, Shauna saw more movement back where she'd first thought she'd seen an animal and knew that he was not alone. This one was making some kind of signal with slow motions of his hand, and it was then that Shauna saw to her chagrin that there were several of them, maybe a dozen in all, spread out over a wide area along the creek banks. All were heavily armed and similarly camouflaged, most carrying camo packs on their backs as well. They looked and moved like soldiers, but that didn't mean they were the good guys, and it certainly didn't make her feel any better about the fact that these men were headed straight up the creek, which would take them directly to Bob Barham's property.

The only positive thing about this unexpected development was that she had seen them first and she was quite certain they had no idea she was there. Whether they already knew about the existence of the cabin or not, she had no idea, but if they continued on the path they were taking, following the stream up, it would be impossible to miss. Shauna was careful not to move or make a sound, other than the slightest adjustments of the rifle so that she could view the men through the scope. Their movements were careful and studied, indicating that they were trained and experienced at this sort of thing. If she'd been at the cabin with the others, they would have all been caught off guard with no warning of their approach.

Shauna needed to warn Jonathan and Vicky, but how? Even though she had seen these men first without being observed, she was already too late. There was no way she could get ahead of them now, as the route up the drainage was a natural funnel that would force her to climb down and work her way along the stream bed because of the impossibly steep slopes between her position and the cabin. She couldn't make it in time, because the point man was already well into the choke point and there was no reasonable way around it that wouldn't get her spotted by those following him. Shauna was stuck, helplessly watching from where she sat hiding until the last of the men passed by on the way up. By then, her only option would be to follow, and what could she do if she did? Once these men discovered the cabin, Jonathan and Vicky would be trapped inside. Shauna was effectively cut off from her companions, and unable to help them unless she could think of something fast.

Seeing these men here today confirmed Shauna's fears that the cabin was not as secluded or safe as Eric Branson may have thought. She was still mad as hell at him for what he'd done, cutting out alone in the middle of the night when they'd all been planning to ride south on Megan's trail together. Eric had left Shauna a letter, detailing his reasoning and trying to explain his decision, but nothing he could have said would have convinced her he was right or mitigated her rage. Shauna had crumpled it up and thrown it in the fireplace in disgust. Eric knew damned well she wouldn't have agreed with splitting up again, especially now that they knew Megan had been with Vicky and Vicky had told them exactly where she was headed with her friend, Aaron. Eric had tried to bring up the idea of going by himself at first, but she'd made it clear to him that such a plan was off the table, and so the bastard went ahead and did it anyway, sneaking out into the night after all the effort the rest of them had put into preparations for the journey.

Eric may have had good reasons for leaving Jonathan and Vicky behind, but not Shauna. She wouldn't slow him down, and after all she'd been through to get here, she felt she should be there when and if he finally caught up to their daughter. Eric had robbed her of that moment though, saying in the letter that his chances of getting through the dangers along the way would be improved if he only had himself to look out for. He had suggested to Vicky when they first got to the cabin that she might be better off to stay behind with Jonathan while he was still recovering from his broken leg, but Megan's former roommate didn't like that idea at all. Eric could have insisted, Shauna now realized, and she could have backed him up on it and maybe then he wouldn't have left her too, but the way he did it, she had no chance to try and change his mind, and that was what irked Shauna the most. She'd dealt with that side of Eric so much during their marriage that it led to their divorce, and now he was pulling the same old stunts. Shauna had stormed out of the cabin that morning after reading the letter, and it had taken an hour of pacing in the early morning chill before she even began to cool off. She'd briefly considered taking off after him, but doing so would require traveling alone, because she wouldn't have a chance of catching up with Jonathan and Vicky in tow. She finally thought better of that idea, and still fuming, made her way back down there to talk to the two of them and figure out how they were going to deal with the prospect of the long and boring wait they were facing. Eric had assured her in his letter that he would be back as soon as possible, but not without Megan. Shauna knew better than to count on such a thing considering all they'd seen though. Anything could happen out there, even to Eric, and maybe even long before he caught up to Megan. And if he did find her, the two of them would be facing the same dangerous journey returning all the way here from northern New Mexico.

No matter how she looked at it, Shauna didn't like any of this, even though she knew deep down that Eric was doing this because he thought it was the best way, and not simply to spite her. His priority really was to catch up to Megan before something bad happened to her, but he had no right to leave Shauna out to do it all himself, putting her in such a terrible and unbearable state of limbo and not knowing once again. There was no telling how long it would take Eric to get to that reservation where Megan was supposed to be, and no guarantee that she was there in the first place. What if she wasn't? What then? Eric had no way of getting a message back to the cabin to let them know. Just how long was she supposed to wait if Eric and Megan didn't show up in a couple of weeks? Two more weeks? Another month? By then the winter snows in the high country would make leaving the cabin extremely difficult and dangerous, if not impossible. The prospect of being trapped there was too much to think about, and every time she did, Shauna wished Eric was standing in front of her so that she could slap the hell out of him.

But the reality was that Eric had been gone more than a week now and it was up to her to figure out how to deal with these armed strangers that would soon be upon the cabin. Shauna couldn't stop them from advancing up that creek bed, not by force, anyway. Even though she'd just had a couple of them in her sights and they had no idea she was there, there were far too many to take out on her own, even if she had more suitable weapons than just a bolt-action hunting rifle and her sidearm. Aside from that, they hadn't proven they were the enemy and for all she knew, they could be legitimate soldiers working to restore order. It was hard to tell the difference these days between the good and the bad and the last thing she wanted to do was fire on them without provocation. Even if she knew for sure they were on the right side though, she wasn't going to walk up and introduce herself and invite them back to the cabin. If they were sweeping the area for possible insurgents, they might open fire first, and even if they didn't, they might force them out of the area due to the problems that had been going on.

Shauna was thinking fast about her limited options as she watched the last of the group slowly work their way through the vegetation surrounding the creek. The best idea she could come up with was to create some kind of diversion to draw their attention away from the cabin before they found it. There was no way to know if it would work or not though, and once committed, she wouldn't be able to second-guess herself if it didn't. It would be up to her to evade and escape if the men took the bait and pursued. If she failed, Jonathan and Vicky were on their own, but they were anyway if she didn't try.

Shauna mentally retraced the route she'd taken down the drainage, thinking about the best place to execute her quickly formulated plan. It wouldn't do to try it now, as the slopes on either side of the creek here were far too steep to allow a quick escape. But there was a smaller intersecting tributary a quarter mile farther up, where she knew the terrain might lend itself to a fast getaway to the north. If she could simply divert their attention to that other natural route, it was possible they'd forget about continuing up the main creek altogether.

Shauna quietly picked her way down among the boulders as she watched the last two men in the party melt into the underbrush upstream and disappear. She had to move quickly enough to keep up with them, but with great caution too. It wouldn't do for them to discover her here, where she'd have no chance of getting away. She paced herself to match their careful, combat-ready advance as she shadowed them, staying far enough back that she only caught occasional glimpses of the last two bringing up the rear of the team as they worked their way upstream. She didn't like that they were spread out so far that she couldn't see all of them, and she hoped her diversion wouldn't result in only some splitting off to follow her, but it was all she could think of given that she was quickly running out of time the nearer they got to the cabin.

As she followed, Shauna ran several scenarios through her head, trying to predict how each would play out. Ideally, she could draw the entire group into pursuit, and if so, she was counting on being able to outdistance them due to her experience and fitness as a runner and her advantage of knowing something of the surrounding area. She was also carrying only a rifle, while they were loaded down with their weapons, spare mags and other supplies in those backpacks. She would be prepared to run as soon as she got their attention, while they were still trying to figure out what was happening, hopefully giving her a good head start. In the best case, the entire team would come after her and she would lose them along the way and then circle back and warn Jonathan and Vicky. The men might still find the cabin eventually, even if she eluded them, but her hope was that it would buy her and her friends enough time to get out of the area and disappear.

Twenty minutes after she began trailing them, Shauna came to the small confluence she remembered, the only easy exit from the main drainage the men were following. The time to act was upon her, and though she was nervous about it, Shauna couldn't afford to hesitate. The options she'd considered for getting the strangers' attention ranged from a simple scream to firing her rifle once or several times to both screaming and firing. The last thing she wanted, of course, was to draw return fire from multiple automatic weapons, so she decided that the option of just firing off gunshots alone wasn't a good idea. She didn't want the men thinking they were under attack. Instead, she wanted to draw their curiosity and encourage them to follow up. Shauna took several deep breaths, checked that her boot laces and the Glock on her side were secure, and then let out the loudest frightened scream she could muster. Ten seconds later, she followed the scream with a shot into the air from the 30.06, the heavy report echoing through the forest and certain to get the attention of everyone in the area. Shauna didn't wait to see the effects of these sounds, however. She turned and jogged a short distance up her escape route, and then paused momentarily to fire off a second round. Then she turned and ran farther.

Whatever the party of men thought of all this, they didn't answer with reactive gunfire, indicating they were indeed disciplined and trained. She doubted they were ignoring it completely however, and when she had created a reasonable distance from where she first began running and had gained higher ground, Shauna stopped one more time, crouching at the base of a large spruce tree to watch and listen. When nothing happened for several minutes, she began to wonder if her tactics had failed completely, but then she saw movement—at least four of the men—slipping rapidly, but cautiously among the trees in her direction, their weapons at ready. Shauna waited just long enough for them to get close enough to catch a glimpse of her when she took off again, sprinting for all she was worth. She knew they had spotted her when she heard a sharp order:

"HEY YOU! STOP RIGHT THERE!" Shauna ignored it and didn't slack up.

"I SAID STOP!" The voice rang out again. She expected to hear bullets ripping through the brush around her at any second, but the shots didn't come, and Shauna put her entire focus into running as fast and far as she could.

Two

JONATHAN COLEMAN STOPPED SUDDENLY at the sound of the first rifle shot, almost losing his balance, but Vicky was right beside him, providing support on the side of his bad leg, and steadying him as he turned in the direction from which it came, far below in the forested drainage, where they knew Shauna was hunting.

"Maybe she got one!" Vicky said. Before he could answer, a second shot came from the same direction. "Or maybe two?"

"Nah, she wouldn't shoot two at one time. She either missed the first shot or wounded him and followed up. We should go see."

"That sounded like it came from a long way off to me, Jonathan. You're doing good to hobble around this far. You don't need to push it. That trail is steep down there, and if you fall again and break your other leg or something, you're going to be totally out of luck."

"We've got Tucker. He can haul me back if I do."

"Yeah, but I can't get you up on his back with two broken legs."

Jonathan knew she was right, but that didn't stop him from wanting to go anyway. He was out here now because he was determined to keep his strength up, and the way he figured it, he needed to start putting a little weight on his leg and using it as much as he dared so it would heal. With Vicky's help, it was feasible to do so. He'd spent all the time he could stand laid up in that cabin. They had made it across the meadow where Bob Barham now lay in the solitary grave they'd dug for him in his favorite spot and were now on the slope above with a nice view back down to the cabin. Jonathan had walked farther this morning than he had since his accident. His leg was getting better, and he expected to make a full recovery just as Bob had said he would when he set and wrapped it.

The weather was nice this morning even though it was still quite cold, and Jonathan was beginning to acclimate to this mountain climate after a lifetime spent in south Florida. He loved the sharp, clean feeling of the air up here, and the scent of the evergreens that made up the bulk of the high elevation forests. Most of all, he liked the silence, broken only by the sound of wind rushing through the tops of the tall spruce and fir trees that surrounded them. It was good to be outside of that cabin and walking among them again, and

Jonathan knew that was why Shauna had gone hunting this morning too, even though they didn't really need the meat.

Being confined to the little cabin was difficult for all of them, but Shauna was especially agitated because of the way Eric left. They had all been preparing for the journey south ever since Eric showed up with Vicky and her information on where Megan was headed. After they buried poor Bob Barham, Jonathan, like Shauna and Vicky had no reason to suspect that Eric would pull the stunt he did. Sure, he'd suggested to Vicky that she might like to stay here at the cabin with Jonathan, saying it was a good option since the journey would be hard, but Vicky would have none of that, insisting she wanted to go and help find her friend. Eric hadn't said any more about it, and they all assumed he was okay with it. At least that way he would have no reason to have to come back here, but even though he helped them all make preparations for leaving, he apparently made a last-minute decision to go alone, slipping out into the night without waking them as they slept.

When Jonathan had opened his eyes to the daylight streaming into the windows that morning, he saw that Eric wasn't in his sleeping bag on the cabin floor, but thought little of it, assuming he was just outside early, getting the horses ready to go. Jonathan had managed to get dressed and get out there while favoring his good leg, eager to see if Eric needed any help, but Eric wasn't in sight, and when he checked the barn where the horses were supposed to be waiting, he didn't find him in there, either. What he *did* find was that two of the animals were gone—Maggie and Sally—the exact two that Eric had already selected for his mount and his pack horse. Jonathan then scanned the dim interior of the barn and saw that Eric's tack and the rest of his gear was missing too. He wondered if maybe Eric had taken the horses and gear on up the trail a bit, while waiting for the rest of them to get ready, but that didn't make sense. It was cold as hell out there at that early hour, far too uncomfortable to be hanging around outside for no good reason. Besides, he'd made no attempt to wake the rest of them if he'd indeed changed his mind and wanted to get an earlier start.

Jonathan had limped his way past the cabin on the crutches Bob had made for him until he reached the creek bed that led up towards the divide. He saw nothing moving among the stands of dense conifers and Eric didn't answer when he called his name out loud several times. Jonathan knew that looking for tracks that close to the cabin was useless, as the snow that remained on the ground there was crisscrossed with foot and hoof prints from their comings and goings doing the daily chores. Picking up Eric's trail, if he'd left one at all, would require going farther up the drainage, but Jonathan was in no shape to do that at the time and so he went back inside to wake Shauna and Vicky.

Shauna had looked at him for a moment with an expression of disbelief on her face before pulling on her boots and storming out the door with her rifle. Jonathan and Vicky were left staring wide-eyed at each other as they listened to her scream Eric's name into the emptiness of the surrounding wilderness. All the frustration and rage she'd ever felt towards the man she'd once loved and later divorced poured out of her into that vastness. But despite her fury, Jonathan had been around her long enough to know that Shauna didn't really hate Eric Branson. After all, he was the man who'd fathered her child, no matter what came between them later, and both of them loved Megan dearly and had put it all on the line to find her. Jonathan had seen glimpses of the fire that still smoldered beneath the surface between the two of them when they were together, and he'd actually expected any day now to see it burst into full-on flames if they remained in such close proximity much longer. No doubt the only thing suppressing it while they were in the cabin was the fact that they weren't alone there. Thinking of it that morning, Jonathan wondered if that were part of the reason Eric had left when he did. Maybe he was averting or postponing the inevitable by simply avoiding it for now?

"Why did Eric even hang around here as long as he did, if this is what he had in mind all along?" Vicky asked. "He could have just left as soon as he brought us here. Why did he get all of us ready for the trip and mislead us into thinking we were all going with him?"

"I don't know if he had it in mind to do that or not, but even if he did, he wouldn't have left right when he got here because first of all he was going to make sure Bob Barham got the proper burial he deserved. Then, he was going to make sure this place was really safe and that we had all the supplies and gear we needed here. But I'll bet he really *was* planning on taking all of us until he got to thinking about it some more; that and seeing how I wasn't able to move worth a crap with this stupid leg! Although knowing what I know of Eric, he may have just changed his mind when he woke up sometime during the night."

"No, it's probably more my fault than yours, Jonathan. Eric didn't want to be bothered with the responsibility of someone else to look after. He wanted me to stay here and he asked me to. I should have agreed to do it. At least then he wouldn't have left Shauna behind."

"You wouldn't slow him down. You've got way more experience riding than any of us, even Shauna. Besides that, you know these mountains from coming out here every summer to stay at your grandpa's ranch. *I'm* the real burden, because out here, in times like these, a guy with a broken leg is useless. I'm lucky I survived it at all, and I damned sure wouldn't have if not for good old Bob Barham. I don't blame you for not wanting to stay alone out here with a cripple."

"Don't be silly, Jonathan. Your leg is healing, and Eric saw that you could ride, even if you couldn't walk or run. He probably thought he'd have to constantly look out for me and protect me because I'm a female the same age as his daughter. I could see why he wouldn't want to deal with that with all his worry about her."

Jonathan certainly wouldn't have minded being stuck in the little cabin alone with Vicky when Eric suggested it, but that had only been a fantasy he didn't really expect to materialize. Now, unless Eric changed his mind again and came back, he *was* stuck here with her though, and unfortunately Eric's very unhappy ex-wife. They heard every word as she vented her anger at first, but though she was still outside somewhere, she'd finally cooled off enough to stop yelling. Of course, she didn't expect Eric to hear it anyway, as he was no doubt already miles away, following the Continental Divide south to New Mexico, but it probably made her feel better to get it out. She would be back in eventually, and before she did, Jonathan decided to hobble over to the wood stove and get it started so he could offer her some coffee. And that was when he found the note.

It was more than a note, really. In fact, it was a letter, and he saw that it was addressed to Shauna, with Eric's signature at the bottom. Jonathan wanted to read it immediately, but he didn't see his name there at the top, so he just turned and showed it to Vicky: "Maybe this will explain it. We'll know when she comes back inside."

"If he took the time to write a full-page letter, then this probably wasn't a last-minute decision. I'm dying to know what it says."

"Me too, but I'm not about to read it. I don't want to do anything to piss Shauna off any more than she already is!"

When she *did* finally come back inside, Jonathan handed Shauna the letter and watched from a safe distance as she scanned the handwritten words on the page.

"That *son of a bitch!* He did this deliberately all right. He left without us to go after Megan on his own!"

"Why would he do it like that?" Vicky asked. "It doesn't make sense."

"Because he's Eric Branson! That's why! Leaving without notice is what he *does!* Why do you think I divorced him ten years ago?"

"Did he say exactly why?" Jonathan was almost afraid to ask, knowing *he* was the most likely reason. "He did it because I would slow all of you down, didn't he?"

"No, he did it because he's a selfish jerk!" Shauna spat.

But Jonathan knew Eric Branson wasn't selfish. Shauna might have reason to think he could be a jerk at times, but he hadn't done all he'd done since Jonathan met him because he was selfish. Everything he did, he did for his daughter and the rest of his family, not to mention the strangers, including himself, that Eric helped along the way when he didn't have to. No, Eric left because he didn't want a crippled Florida punk slowing him down. His priority was to catch up to Megan now that he knew where she'd gone, and he wasn't going to do anything that would compromise that mission. Jonathan totally got it. He really did. It was the kind of thing he would expect Eric to do after getting to know him over the past several weeks. Even if not for Jonathan's injury, Eric could travel faster and stealthier without the three of them tagging along, and simply leaving without telling them was the only way he could do that. Shauna would have never agreed to it, as she had already shot down the idea when Eric casually brought it up. It sucked to think that Eric didn't trust even him enough to let him in on his plans, but Jonathan figured Eric wasn't taking any chances. Once he made up his mind to do something, he didn't second-guess himself, and he probably didn't want to hear any objections or arguments from anyone, even if he believed Jonathan was on his side in this.

"He thinks I'm going to just sit here in this cabin for God knows how long while he follows our daughter all the way to New Mexico? I'll have no way of knowing if he ever gets there or not or if he finds Megan when he does! It could be weeks before he gets back here with her, and I'm supposed to just sit here and *wait?* That's just crazy!"

"He wouldn't have done it if I didn't have this broken leg. I'm sorry I was so stupid that day, Shauna. This is all my fault."

"No, it's my fault!" Vicky said. "I shouldn't be here. Eric didn't want to take me to New Mexico and he didn't want to leave me here alone either. I just created another problem for him by being here. I'm so sorry, Shauna."

"It's not your fault, Vicky. And it's not yours either, Jonathan. It's just Eric! He thinks he knows better than everybody. He can't stop us from following him though. We know the way he went."

"Maybe, but we'll never catch up to him if he doesn't want us to," Jonathan said, "not with me slowing you down. I'd say go on without me, but I don't think it's a good idea for the two of you to be traveling these mountains alone. Even the three of us, for that matter. Without Eric, we'd be an easy target for an ambush. Maybe we ought to just chill like he said. Maybe he *will* get there faster, and it won't take all that long for him to get back here with Megan."

Shauna didn't want to hear it, but Jonathan knew that deep down, she agreed. Out here in the vastness of these mountains, there was no guarantee they'd ever find Eric if they tried to follow, especially if he got new information regarding Megan and headed somewhere other than the reservation. And if the three of them left on their own, Eric would then have to look for them when he returned here either with or without Megan. Considering all this, Shauna finally accepted that they might as well wait for now, but she was in a terrible mood those first few days, and Jonathan knew that if enough time passed without Eric's return, she would be determined to press on in search of Megan anyway. In the meantime, she had taken to hunting and exploring the area surrounding the cabin, and each day when she left, it was a relief to Jonathan and Vicky, as tension when she was around was palpable.

"I think she'll chill out soon enough," Vicky had said after Shauna left that morning with the deer rifle. She hadn't mentioned Eric's name for a couple of days, and they both knew she was making an effort not to think about him.

"It's obvious she's still in love with him," Vicky said. I don't care how mad she gets or that she divorced him and married someone else. I can see it in the way she looks at him."

"Yeah, you're probably right."

"I know I am. He probably doesn't even know it though. Guys are stupid like that."

"Is that right?" Jonathan asked, momentarily meeting her gaze before quickly looking away again. He wished Vicky had thoughts like that about him that maybe he was just too stupid to pick up on, but he doubted that was the case. They'd just met, and what would she see in him anyway? He sure wouldn't have been her type before all these events went down, her being a college student and all, and now, in a world that required men that could do useful things like the fishing and shooting he was good at, he had a bum leg and couldn't do jack shit. But whether Vicky saw anything in him or not, it had been hard for Jonathan to keep his eyes off her during the past couple of weeks since she'd arrived here with Shauna and Eric. Even if he wasn't her type, she'd been talkative and pleasant to be around. And she'd insisted on helping him with his recovery, walking at his side to steady him as he gradually began relying less and less on his crutches.

And now today, with her help, he'd walked farther from the cabin than he'd been since he arrived here. Sure, she'd led Tucker along as back up to get him back if something happened, but Jonathan had managed just fine without needing the horse. All-in-all, it had been an amazing morning, taking in the grandeur of the unspoiled mountain wilderness while being guided and assisted by a beautiful young woman that he had a hard time keeping his eyes off of. The rifle shots that interrupted them were an intrusion into that perfection, but he knew they might also mean they would soon have a welcome change of diet.

"Let's just ease along that way a little, if you don't mind helping me, Vicky. I can't wait to find out if she got one or not. If she did, she'll be coming back to get one of the horses and she'll need your help too, I'm sure."

"Yeah, but if she missed those shots, she'll be coming back in a bad mood and you know it. It might be better if we are still here, out of her way, just in case. Look, I've been down that way, and it gets steep down there in a hurry. I don't think you should try it yet. Let's just sit down and wait right here where we can watch for her. We'll know before she makes it to the cabin whether she's had good luck or bad."

Jonathan didn't really like that idea, but as long as Vicky was sitting there beside him, he wasn't going to complain. They found a smooth rock that was just the right height to make a comfortable perch at the foot of a large outcrop, while Tucker waited nearby. They were talking quietly as they sat there until some twenty minutes later, when Vicky got up to go give Tucker a pat. It was while she was over there that Jonathan spotted movement down near the creek a couple hundred yards below, and he saw immediately that it wasn't Shauna. Jonathan turned and quickly shushed Vicky with a whisper: "Don't move Vicky! Stay where you are and keep Tucker quiet!"

She looked at him in confusion and he pointed in the direction he'd been watching. A man dressed in camo and carrying an assault rifle was standing out in the open now and making some kind of signaling motion with his free hand. And moments later, Jonathan saw several other figures materialize from the forest behind him.

Three

NOW THAT SHE KNEW they'd seen her, Shauna ran as fast as she could without looking back, wanting to put as much distance between herself and the group of armed men as possible. Fortunately, the heavy forest through which she was running meant she didn't have to stay all that far ahead of them to keep out of sight. They hadn't fired any shots yet, but that didn't mean they wouldn't if she presented them with an easy target, so she couldn't let up. She already knew they were coming after her because after she ignored his shouted order to stop, she glanced briefly over her shoulder and saw the same man waving his followers in her direction. It was what she'd wanted when she screamed and fired her rifle, but now that she'd actually gotten their attention, Shauna wondered if she'd made a mistake. It would have been easy to stay out of sight and simply follow them back to the cabin, but then what? With no reasonable way to get ahead of them, she couldn't have warned Jonathan and Vicky in time and there were far too many of them to confront. No, this was better, but now that the chase was on, she couldn't help but feel fear.

Shauna knew she couldn't afford to make a misstep and fall, so though her body was flooded with adrenalin as she sprinted, she held back just enough to give herself time to pick the best line through the many obstacles of roots, fallen logs and rocks that the challenging terrain presented.

The heavy hunting rifle was a burden to her now, as she had no intention of using it against her pursuers, but she didn't dare leave it either, in case she had no choice in the end. She ran with it in her hands as that was safer than slinging it on her back where the barrel might snag a branch and trip her up. Her Glock was her last line of defense beyond the rifle, but Shauna sure hoped it wouldn't come to a standoff like that, because it was doubtful she'd survive it. She had counted thirteen men in the patrol, or raiding party or whatever it was, but she couldn't be sure she had even seen them all in the heavy timber of the drainage. She also had no way of knowing if all of them were coming after her, or if some had waited behind or even continued on, in the direction of the cabin. She didn't want to think about the latter, because that would mean her diversion had already failed whether she escaped or not.

Despite her high level of fitness and endurance, Shauna was breathing hard before she'd covered even half a mile. The streambed route that was her only option began climbing immediately from where it intersected the main drainage and running up a grade at that already high elevation was grueling.

Shauna could only hope it was harder on her pursuers than it was on her and that they would soon give up. But she soon encountered a new problem as she entered an area where the trees thinned out and the forest became more open. Here, the exposed ground was completely covered with a light layer of snow. There were patches of snow and ice along the main creek she'd just left too, especially in the deep shade, but there they weren't so big they couldn't be avoided. Up here, there was no way around it and no way around leaving tracks in it. She had no time to make an effort to hide them either. What was worse was that it went on like that for as far as she could see ahead. That gave another advantage to her pursuers, as they would be able to follow her even if they couldn't keep up. Shauna doubted she would break free of the snow until she could work her way up and over the ridge to the warmer side that was exposed to the morning sun. She glanced back over her shoulder again after she'd crossed a hundred yards of the stuff and to her dismay, saw three of the camo-clad men loping relentlessly through the trees on her trail, like hungry wolves running down their prey. *Maybe she'd underestimated them? Were these men not only soldiers, but perhaps members of some kind of highly-trained Special Forces unit like Eric had been in?* If they were, they wouldn't give up as easily as she'd hoped, and probably not at all. Shauna briefly reconsidered her options. Pausing to fire a round from the rifle might stop them for a moment, and cause them to seek

31

cover, but then what? She couldn't run and stay in concealment the entire time. One of them would eventually get a clear shot at her, and that would be the end of it. They might do that anyway, but since they hadn't fired yet, she figured they must not want her dead.

Shauna dug in again and sprinted for all she was worth, determined to lose those three before they had a chance to close in further. But the terrain was working against her and the way led up an even steeper slope that reduced her pace to little more than a fast hike. Worse yet, she was caught out in the open with no cover or concealment. She gave it everything she had, but Shauna couldn't reach the top of that exposed slope before the men behind her arrived at a place that gave them an unobstructed view. Shauna flinched and then stumbled as she heard the sudden staccato burst of automatic rifle fire behind her and saw the impact of bullets striking the powder just above her head. She had nowhere to go but down to the ground, where she tried to flatten herself as low as possible, knowing even as she did so that she was still an easy target. But when she stopped, the firing stopped too as suddenly as it had started. Shauna breathed out again, surprised she wasn't hit. Unlike that day during the firefight offshore in the Gulf when she'd felt the searing pain of a bullet ripping through her hand and arm, she felt nothing but the adrenalin. She thought maybe another burst was coming, but when it didn't, she risked a glance back at the men and saw that the one that had fired his weapon still had her in his sights, while two of his companions were spreading out and advancing in her direction. Behind those three, she could now see two more of their party that had just caught up to them. Shauna's run was finished, and there was nothing she could do but wait and see what they were going to do now that they had her at their mercy. To do otherwise would be suicide, and she knew it. Shauna moved her hands to the top of her head where they could see them as she waited for the two that approached to close in. Both of them had their weapons trained on her as well, and she had no choice but to comply with their orders.

"KEEP YOUR HANDS WHERE THEY ARE AND DON'T MOVE!" One of the men said as he circled to one side, while his companion moved to the other flank. Her rifle was in the snow beside her where she'd dropped it and the Glock was clearly visible on her belt, as she'd made no attempt to draw it.

"Don't shoot! I'm not moving!"

"Roll over, face down! But keep your hands on top of your head where I can see them!"

Shauna did as she was ordered and a moment later the second man was on top of her, pinning her down in the snow with a knee in the small of her back as he yanked the Glock out of her holster and tossed the rifle out of reach. Then, moving to one side, he pulled her hands down behind her back and held them together as he reached for something in his pocket. Shauna struggled and tried to pull her hands free, but by then, the man's companion was there beside him as well, and she heard more voices as the others closed in. Seconds later, she felt her wrists constricted as she heard the unmistakable clicking of a plastic zip tie cinched into place around them.

"What are you doing? Let me go!"

"You're under arrest! Stop resisting or it will be harder than it has to be."

"Under arrest for what? I haven't done anything wrong! Who are you people? What right do you have to arrest anyone out here?"

"You're under arrest for suspicion of terrorism and armed insurrection!"

"I'm not a terrorist! Are you insane? I'm an American citizen."

"I'm not interested in your citizenship. You're illegally in possession of weapons in an insurgent occupied zone. But more relevant, you just fired one of those weapons at authorized government contractors."

"What are you talking about? I haven't fired a weapon at anyone!"

"Other than the two rounds back there where you tried to ambush our patrol along that creek?"

"I wasn't firing at any of you! I didn't even know you were there. I was deer hunting in the area when I happened upon a big black bear at close range and surprised it. I screamed at it, hoping to scare it away, and when that didn't work, I fired my rifle to make more noise! The bear stopped coming towards me, but I had to fire a second time before it ran off. When it did, I wanted to get out of there as fast as I could. I had no idea anyone else was around until I heard someone yelling at me, and then I saw the bunch of you in camouflage running towards me with guns. I ran because I didn't know who you were, and I was scared!"

"A bear?" The man chuckled and turned to his companion. "We haven't seen any bears, have we Mullins?"

"No sir! That sounds like a bullshit story to me, Chief."

"It's *not* bullshit!" Shauna said. "These mountains are full of bears. Anyone should know that!"

"Maybe so but forget about the bear. I just want to know how many of you there are up here, and where your base of operations is located."

"There's no one up here with me and there is no 'base'!" Shauna said. "I'm alone."

"Do you really expect me to believe you're alone way up here? A woman, in these mountains by yourself? It's dropping below zero up here at night this time of year. Where are you staying and what are you eating? It doesn't look like that deer rifle is doing you much good, but then you don't look like you're starving either. Now, one more time, how many are with you and where are they?"

Shauna was trying to read the man before she answered. He'd mentioned 'government contractors' and she knew all too well that could cover a lot of territory, but at least if it were true, they probably weren't part of a rogue militia or band of insurgents themselves. They seemed professional and highly skilled, so it seemed likely that this man his companion had called "Chief" might be telling the truth, but that didn't mean she was ready to trust them. They weren't giving *her* the benefit of the doubt, running her down and restraining her as they had, and telling her she was under arrest for terrorism. She simply couldn't risk bringing the same fate to Jonathan and Vicky, knowing as she did from hearing all of Eric's stories that some of these contractors operated with completely different rules of engagement than regular military. That of course, was why they were often used in situations and places where rules were a serious hindrance to getting things done. And Eric should know, because he spent years working for such outfits himself, although he'd avoided the dirtiest of them. Shauna knew she had to think of something to buy more time and divert their attention elsewhere, and the only place that came to mind was the ranch that had belonged to Vicky's grandparents.

"I was staying with a friend of my daughter's, at her grandfather's ranch until a gang of looters came and stole their horses, and then murdered them and burned their house down," Shauna said. "I was the only survivor, and only because I was out hunting that day like I am now. I heard the shooting and headed back there as fast as I could. But I saw the men that did it from the ridge overlooking the place and I knew there was nothing I could do, so I stayed up there until they were gone. When I finally went down there, I saw that my daughter's friend and her grandparents were dead. It was terrible, but there was nothing I could have done. Look, I was there because I was looking for my daughter. I'd hoped to find her there with her friend, but she didn't know where she was, and I was out of options."

The men looked at her with little expression as she told her story, and Shauna could tell they didn't find it very convincing. "A ranch house, huh? Where was this, exactly? We haven't seen a ranch house anywhere nearby. This is all national forest wilderness land."

"It's to the south. Not all that far really. Less than a two-day hike down the Divide Trail, and then a short way west on the first gravel road you come to."

"And you just struck out into the mountains by yourself after this happened, and that's how you ended up here?"

"What else could I do? I couldn't stay there. I didn't know if those men were coming back or not."

Before he could answer, the man questioning her was interrupted by one of his team members, who'd been standing guard off to one side, but was now walking quickly towards them, a handheld radio up to his ear. "They found something, Chief. About two klicks farther up that creek we were on. It's a cabin. Way off the grid and pretty well hidden."

"Is it occupied? Did they encounter any resistance?"

"No sir! Reece says they secured the perimeter first, and then cleared it. They didn't find anyone inside, but there were lots of weapons and other supplies in there, and some horses outside. He said someone's living there for sure. The wood stove inside was still hot."

"Tell him to get an inventory of all the weapons and ammunition and keep the property secured until we get there. I want to see this place myself and I've got one of the occupants with me now."

"Rodger. I'll pass the word."

When the "chief" turned back to her, Shauna was shaking her head. "I don't know anything about a cabin like that." She'd heard enough of the conversation to know that for whatever reason, the men who'd discovered the cabin didn't have Jonathan and Vicky. It surprised her really, to hear that, because she thought surely they would either be inside or close enough by if outside that they would have been seen when those men found the place. But however the two of them managed to elude capture, Shauna was elated to hear it, and she wasn't going to give these men any information that might compromise them or cause them to add more false accusations to the reasons they were detaining her.

"I don't know anything about a cabin up that way, but I haven't been all the way up there. I've been trying to keep out of the higher elevations because it's so cold."

"We'll see about that. I'll bet you'll recognize the stash of weapons my men found when we get there, and I'm sure whoever's with you will be back home soon. Now get up! Let's go!"

Shauna got to her knees and then stood, unable to dust the snow off her jacket and pants with her hands secured behind her back. She stomped her feet to shake some of it off as one of the other men picked up her Glock and stashed it in his backpack.

"What do you want me to do with this, Chief?" The same man asked, holding up the 30.06.

"Break it and leave it here. We have no use for it."

"You have no right to confiscate and destroy my guns!" Shauna said. "That rifle is my only means of getting food, and the pistol is for personal protection."

"You're not going to need either now. And yes, we do have the right and the orders to confiscate firearms from all civilians we encounter with them. It's nothing personal, but I'm being paid to do a job."

The man with the Remington emptied the chamber and magazine and then walked over to a large rock, against which he smashed the buttstock, breaking it off at the receiver. He then wedged the barrel into a crevice in the rock and leaned into it with all his weight, bending it enough to render it useless. Then Shauna was forced to start walking, flanked on either side by two of the five who'd ran her down while the other three pushed on ahead, anxious to see what their other teammates had found. Shauna had no idea what they planned to do when they got there, and she was out of ideas for plotting an escape.

At this point, she was mostly willing to believe the men were who they said they were—a team of private contractors. That didn't necessarily mean they were really working for the U.S. government, but it seemed likely that they were, as they seemed highly disciplined and professional. It would make sense that most of them, like Eric, were probably former Special Forces operatives now working in the private sector for better pay and flexibility. Shauna noted that their weapons and equipment were top-tier, but though they were all more or less dressed in tactical camouflage, they weren't wearing any cohesive or official-looking uniform.

What all of this would mean for her now, she wasn't sure, but Shauna felt somewhat better that at least she hadn't fallen into the hands of a band of insurrectionists or outright outlaws, which would be far worse. She would have been willing to divulge more of the truth about her presence here though if her captors were members of an actual military unit that operated through the normal chain of command. In that case, she might be able to use her recent interactions with Lieutenant Holton back east to her advantage. As it was though, Shauna decided to keep quiet for now and say as little as possible, at least until they arrived at the cabin and she knew the status of Jonathan and Vicky and what these men planned to do next. If it turned out that they had them and she couldn't deny they'd been staying there, she hoped to convince them that she and her companions were in no way involved with any activities related to the troublemakers that roamed these mountains. But considering all the weapons that were indeed stashed at Bob Barham's cabin, both his own and the ones they'd brought there with them, she wasn't optimistic that story would go over very well.

The steep hike back up there was difficult with her hands behind her back, and the two men flanking her offered no help, other than urging her to move faster. When they finally emerged at the lower end of the meadow that extended down from the cabin, Shauna saw that the men had thrown almost everything that was inside out on the ground. She looked, but didn't see Jonathan or Vicky among them, and wondered how they'd managed to escape capture. Then she glanced over at the horses that were all hitched together to the post outside the barn, no doubt secured there by the intruders. Tucker wasn't among them! Shauna smiled inwardly, hoping for the best, but knowing that wherever Jonathan and Vicky may have gone, they may return at any moment, unaware that they were riding straight into a trap.

Four

JONATHAN'S HEART POUNDED AS he watched the armed strangers in disbelief. They had simply appeared out of nowhere and without warning at the lower edge of the meadow, and now they were spreading out on both sides, just inside the tree line, obviously intent on surrounding the cabin. He wasn't sure if he'd seen them all or not, but he counted at least eight. How they'd found Bob's place, he had no idea, but watching the cautious way they were moving into position around it, Jonathan was glad he and Vicky weren't inside right now. These strangers were up to no good, Jonathan was certain, and from what he could see, they had come there to raid the place or remove the occupants.

He saw the other horses down there in the meadow acting skittish because of the intruders, and Jonathan turned slowly and looked back to where Vicky was standing next to Tucker, soothing him with whispers as she gently patted him to keep him quiet. Vicky was wide-eyed with fear as she looked back at him. He knew she was wondering what was going on down there, and she needed to see this.

"Take Tucker a little farther back in the trees and tie him there," he whispered. "And bring the rifle when you come back."

He had Bob's .44 Magnum revolver on his belt, but a handgun would do them little good if those men armed with rifles spotted them and started shooting. He'd also brought the .45-70 lever-action, carried in the scabbard attached to Tucker's saddle. Vicky had it with her as she crept slowly back to his side.

"I counted eight of them! There may be more though. They've basically surrounded the cabin from within the edge of the woods."

"What do you think they want?"

"Probably everything we've got! What else?"

Before Vicky could say anything, her response was cut short by a burst of automatic gunfire, somewhere far off in the distance in the direction from which they'd heard the two rifle shots earlier. "That sounds like it came from the same place Shauna was shooting!" Vicky said.

"If it was her that we heard the first time, yes! Either way, that is the direction she went this morning, down the creek, and she didn't have one of the M4s or AKs with her. There must be even more of those jokers than I thought!"

"What are we going to do, Jonathan? Shauna could be in trouble!"

"I know she could! She probably is! We've got to figure out a way to get down there and find her if we can, but we can't let these guys see us."

"Look! They're doing something down there right now!"

Jonathan turned his gaze back to the view of the cabin and saw two men running from the edge of the woods to the front porch, converging on it from opposite sides. When they flattened themselves against the log walls on either side of the door, he knew what was coming next. He saw some of the other men in the tree line ready their rifles as they covered their two buddies, and then one of the men on the porch backed up and drove a hard front kick into the door. It wouldn't have given way so easily if anyone had been inside to drop the massive wooden bar that Bob Barham had fashioned into place, but that lock wasn't designed to be used from outside, and the smaller latch Jonathan had secured gave way easily to the man's vicious kick. As soon as it did, the two men entered the doorway with their weapons at ready while two more sprinted from the woods to provide close-in backup. Eric had told Jonathan stories of using similar tactics clearing buildings in the war zones where he'd fought, and when Jonathan didn't hear any gunfire, he figured these men were trained professionals. Inexperienced amateurs would have sprayed rounds indiscriminately, out of fear, even before they determined if the structure was occupied or not.

"Dammit!" Jonathan said. "Those bastards are going to find all our shit! They're going to clean us out! Our food... our weapons... everything!"

"I don't see that we can stop them, Jonathan. There are way too many of them!"

"Not if Eric were here, there wouldn't be, but he isn't, so yeah, you're right. Man, we are *so* screwed if we lose all our stuff!"

"Maybe they won't take it," Vicky said. "Maybe they're looking for someone, and they got the wrong place. Do you think they could be soldiers? They look like they could be to me."

"Maybe, but I'm not willing to let them know we're here so we can ask them. They seem to know what they're doing, but that doesn't mean they wouldn't shoot us on sight. We need to try and slip out of here before they start looking around, because now that they're inside the cabin, they're gonna know that someone's been living there. If they come up this way and I'm still here, I'm screwed, because I can't run. Besides, we need to find another way down to where we heard that shooting and see if we can find Shauna."

"There is a way on the other side of the ridge above us, if we can find a route that Tucker can handle. There's no way I could help you walk that far as steep is it is, but Tucker could carry you while I lead him. Shauna and I were up there just the other day. It looked like another small creek down in the ravine on the other side, and she said it had to run into the main creek somewhere."

"Then that's the way we need to go, but we're going to have to be real careful slipping away from where we are right now, especially with Tucker. He'd be easy to spot from down there if they start glassing these slopes, and he may get agitated and make noise. Go ahead and lead him a bit farther back in the woods and wait for me there. I'm going to watch these guys just a moment longer and then I'll crawl back over there and mount up."

"You should come now, Jonathan. Why wait?"

"Because I want to see what they're going to do when they finish searching. I want to make sure they don't just leave afterwards, because if they do, we might have other options."

"I wouldn't count on it, Jonathan."

"I'm not, and I won't be long. Now go! Take it slow and keep that horse quiet!"

Vicky did as she was told, and Jonathan turned his attention back to the men raiding Bob Barham's cabin. He now saw that three of them had discovered the old man's grave out there in the meadow, and were standing there looking at it, no doubt reading the inscription on the wooden marker that bore the recent date of his passing. He knew it wouldn't fool them into thinking no one still lived there though, because there were dirty dishes in the sink and the coals in the wood stove hadn't even had time to burn out since breakfast. Jonathan then saw a couple of the others that had been inside come out onto the porch carrying the rifles and shotguns they'd found in there. They leaned them against the railing and went back for more. After several trips, they had stacked the ammo cans and the bags containing magazines and the handguns out there as well. Jonathan knew it must have looked to them like whoever lived there had an arsenal and was seriously prepared for anything, and it was the truth. However, all those preparations had done them little good in the end, as they had been caught out and surprised by this silent and swift-moving band of invaders, who had now taken possession of it all without firing a shot.

As he watched them, Jonathan noticed one man walking towards two of the others while holding something up to his ear. It was hard to be sure at that distance, but Jonathan figured it was a radio of some kind. He already knew there were more of the men than just those he could see at the cabin because of that burst of gunfire. Jonathan thought it quite likely that the one he saw with the radio was in contact with the rest. They would probably be coming here as well, and soon, so Jonathan knew it was time to get moving if he and Vicky were to avoid getting caught. He feared the worst for Shauna if she had indeed exchanged gunfire with any of this crew. She was far outnumbered and outgunned and had likely been as surprised as he and Vicky at their sudden arrival. All he and Vicky could do was try and find her down there in the direction from which they heard the shooting, but they had to be extremely careful to avoid being seen while doing so.

Jonathan crawled quietly back to where Vicky was waiting with Tucker. With her standing beside him, so he could put an arm around her while hanging onto the saddle horn with his other hand, Jonathan was able to get his good foot into the stirrup, and from there, swing his injured leg up and over. She passed the .45-70 lever action rifle up to him and then he was ready to go. "Just take it real slow and stop ever so often to listen," he said, as she took the reins in one hand and began walking quietly in front of Tucker. "Try to keep to the heaviest cover that we can get through with Tucker. We don't know that some of the others with them aren't out here combing the woods already."

The going was difficult as Vicky sought a suitable route up and over the ridge. She had to double back in places, taking advantage of the natural switchbacks she could find, and the higher they went, the more snow accumulation they encountered. Jonathan hated that they were leaving a visible trail in it, but there was little they could do about that now. At least it didn't start from the cabin, as the meadow and surrounding areas down there were mostly free of snow until the next storm came through. Jonathan hoped that would buy them some time, as the men wouldn't pick up the trail until they had time to expand their search radius well away from the cabin. Whether they would even do that or not, there was no way of knowing, but it was best to assume they would. Though he and Vicky stopped several times to listen carefully, they could no longer hear the men down at the cabin from up there where they were, and there was nothing else from the direction they'd heard that machine gun burst either.

Vicky at last found a way over the crest of the ridge and without pausing on the top, began picking a way down the other side that Tucker could negotiate. All of this was unfamiliar territory to Jonathan, but Vicky whispered back to him that she was sure it was the same way she'd gone with Shauna a few days before, and that she was certain they would find the smaller stream somewhere down in the forested ravine below. As he hung on to the saddle horn while Tucker descended, Jonathan realized that Vicky's insistence on bringing the horse with them that morning had made all the difference. Jonathan had said it wasn't necessary and that the purpose of going out there was to work on building up his strength, but Vicky argued that she couldn't carry him back to the cabin if he couldn't make it, and besides, it was no trouble to bring Tucker along, even though they were walking. Now, having the horse could mean the difference in life or death, because Jonathan knew he wouldn't get far without him, even if his leg was getting better.

Aside from his concern over whether the intruders had already found Shauna, Jonathan doubted there'd be anything left to go back to at the cabin, not that they'd ever feel safe there again if there was. From what he'd seen of the way those men were ransacking it, piling everything up outside, he fully expected to lose everything, and probably the remaining horses as well. Taking inventory of what little they had with them, it was practically nothing: no food, no extra clothing, and little in the way of weapons and essential gear. The heavy-caliber lever-action rifle was a good hunting weapon and good for defense against large, dangerous animals, like bears, but with only a 5-round internal magazine, it was hardly suitable for combat against modern firearms. The Magnum revolver he carried was pretty much the same, while back at the cabin there were several assault rifles and high-capacity semi-automatic pistols, along with lots of magazines and ammo for most of them. All of that was out of reach now though, but at least he and Vicky had escaped with their lives—for now. Seeing the way those men breached the cabin door as if they were in house-to-house combat, Jonathan thought it just as likely they would have been shot on sight as taken prisoner, had the two of them been inside at the time. Whatever was happening at the cabin now though, was beyond their control. Finding Shauna was the important thing, and as they descended down into the drainage of the smaller tributary, Jonathan could only hope they weren't too late to help her.

Vicky stopped when they came into view of the small stream rushing over the rocks a hundred feet below. "This is it, Jonathan. It runs into the main creek about a mile farther down," she whispered.

"I think we're close to where that shooting was coming from. We've got to be extra careful from here on."

"Yep, and that's why you need to wait here with Tucker and let me go on ahead. I can move a lot quieter by myself."

"It's too dangerous to go alone, Vicky! We'll tie Tucker up and leave him here. I can make it."

"You can't be serious, Jonathan! You'll either have to use your crutches or lean on me. Either way is way too slow and will probably make too much noise. And what happens if we need to run? You can't! I'm not going far, I just want to quietly climb down to the creek bank and look around. It looks like there's plenty of snow down there. If Shauna was down there, there'll be footprints. Give me the revolver and you wait here with the rifle to cover me. Believe me, I'll hide if I see anyone other than Shauna moving down there. And I'll be back here as fast as I can."

Jonathan didn't like it, but hearing her logic, there was little he could argue with. It sucked to be injured like he was, and every day since it happened, he thought about how stupid he'd been to slip and fall like he did. The broken leg had been a pain in the ass for him and everyone else that had to deal with him. Now he had to sit here and wait while Vicky did the dangerous job of reconnoitering ahead in a situation where she could run into a group of armed goons that she wouldn't have a chance against alone. But they had to try to find Shauna at all cost. Even if they lost everything in the cabin and had to leave the area, if the three of them escaped with their lives they would find a way to overcome the setback and do whatever they had to do next.

As he watched Vicky work her way through the trees down the slope, Jonathan whispered quietly to Tucker to keep him settled down. Jonathan knew little of horses before arriving here in Colorado, but since his fall, when Bob Barham used one to move him safely down to his cabin, he'd learned the value of the animals that now played a huge role in his life. Vicky was an expert with them, and she had assured him that Tucker was smart and well-trained, and that he knew what to do, regardless of Jonathan's inexperience. She had been giving him riding tips for days now, usually out in the meadow in front of the cabin, and the more time Jonathan spent on the horses, the more he liked it. He'd also savored the time he got to spend with her, although he doubted anything would come of it. She was being nice to him and helping him because they'd been cast together into a situation where helping each other was essential to survival.

And he felt he was mainly on the receiving end of all that help, and it aggravated him to no end that he couldn't be more useful, especially in a crisis like the one they were facing today. He was nervous when she disappeared from sight, and time seemed to drag by while she was gone. But then he saw her making her way quietly up out of the ravine. Shauna wasn't with her, but Vicky was carrying something in her hand.

"I found it jammed into a crack between two boulders," she said, as she handed the ruined deer rifle to Jonathan. It was the Remington hunting rifle of Bob's that Shauna had left with that morning; Jonathan had recognized it instantly, because he had been looking forward to trying it out himself. Now, with a broken stock and bent barrel, the rifle was useless, but Jonathan was surprised to see that the scope was still intact. It could be removed and would be useful by itself, and he would do so before discarding the ruined weapon. "There were lots of footprints all around where I found it," Vicky explained, "but they didn't go any further up this way. It looked like whoever made them went back the other way, down towards the main creek. I looked everywhere nearby, afraid I might find a body, but there was nothing."

Jonathan felt his stomach tighten into knots as he thought about what might have become of Shauna. "Did you see any blood in the snow? Any other evidence that she may have been hit by whoever fired those rounds?"

"No, I thought of that too, but I didn't see any. I think they must have caught her somehow and taken the gun away from her. They must have her now, Jonathan! I wanted to keep going to see, but I didn't want to leave you here wondering. But now I'm thinking I need to sneak back up to the other side of that ridge, where I can see the cabin again and see if they brought her back there. We have to know, Jonathan."

"I agree, but you can't do it alone. I'm going with you!"

"You can't, Jonathan! There's nothing you can do, because you can't go on foot, and if we try and take Tucker back over there, there's a good chance we'll be seen. You said yourself that they're going to know that the cabin was lived in. They're probably going to be looking everywhere for us, and when they come, we've got to be ready to make a quick getaway. You've got to trust me on this, Jonathan. I just want to get one more look and see if I can spot Shauna. We have to know if they have her or not!"

Five

As she was led onto Bob Barham's property, Shauna acted as if she'd never seen any of it before. Even though she'd noted Tucker's absence from among the other horses, she made sure not to focus on any one area or to show any obvious interest to indicate she cared about any of it. She could see that the others that found the place while the five chased her down had already gone through the cabin and hauled out almost everything that was inside. They seemed more interested in the weapons than anything else, and when the one they'd been calling "Chief" saw the stash they'd stacked outside, he grabbed Shauna roughly by the arm and pulled her over to the side of the porch, where two of the men were taking an inventory of the guns and ammunition.

"Where did you people get all of this stuff, and what were you planning to do with it?" He demanded of her.

"I have no idea who these guns belong to! I told you, I'm not with anyone out here. I was at the ranch I told you about because I was looking for my daughter. I've never been here in my life!" She thought she sounded convincing, but when she looked at him again, the chief wasn't looking at her, instead, he was staring at something amid the assorted pile of weapons, something that seemed to really pique his interest. "Hand me that rifle case, Jenkins! The brown one."

When the other man passed it to him, Shauna felt a knot twisting in her stomach. She knew what it was, and so did the chief.

"Remington!" He said, as his eyes burned into hers with accusation. "It says Remington right here on the front of this case, but it sure feels awfully light for a rifle case! Let's see what we have inside!"

He opened up the case and of course, found it empty. It was the case for Bob Barham's Remington Model 700, and he knew as well as she did, even before he pulled out the owner's manual Bob had tucked into an inner compartment, that the weapon that had been stored in there was the same as the 30.06 they'd taken from Shauna when they apprehended her.

"You have some explaining to do, lady, and this time, you'd better shoot straight. I don't have any more time for games."

Before she could say anything, one of the other men that arrived there first interrupted: "Chief, I think that rifle and some of the other nice hunting pieces we found here probably belonged to the owner of this cabin. We found his grave right out front, down there past the horse barn; freshly dug. This woman and her accomplices probably killed him."

Shauna's mind was racing as she considered how to respond to this. It was useless to continue denying that she'd been staying in the cabin, but since these men didn't seem to know about Jonathan and Vicky and since the two of them obviously weren't here, she wasn't about to volunteer any information about them. She settled instead for a half-truth, as she knew she had to give them a lot more than she already had, because the rifle case had already proven she was hiding something from them.

"Okay look, I *have* been staying here. You know that now, but surely you understand why I wouldn't volunteer that information. I have no idea who you people are, no matter what you said. You're holding me against my will, and all I know is that these mountains are full of some very bad people."

"There are bad people out here indeed," the chief said, glancing out at the solitary grave marker in the meadow. "And it's hard to say who they are."

"Bob Barham was the owner of this cabin. He built it as his mountain retreat long before everything in this country started falling apart. He wasn't murdered though. His death was an unfortunate accident. My husband and I buried him. He was helping us out, because like I said, my daughter is missing. Both of us came here looking for her, and it's true what I told you about that ranch. It's also true that the owners of that place were murdered by looters or bandits, whatever you want to call them. But before it happened, we found out from them where our daughter was headed. It's a long way from here and Bob Barham was going to help us get there before he died, but it didn't work out. So, my husband left me up here because he felt it was safer for me to stay here than to travel all that way through the mountains with him. We both felt this place was secluded enough that no one would find it, and they haven't, until you came along today.

"You said you and your men are contractors working for the U.S. military. I found that interesting, because my husband has worked in that field for years, mostly in the Middle East and Europe, but he was a SEAL team operator before that. We had a lot of help getting out here to Colorado because of his former military service. In fact, he participated in a rescue operation for the Army in exchange for their help getting us here. That's where some of the weapons you see came from. They are not stolen, and he would never have anything to do with the insurgents or terrorist groups that are causing all the problems in this country. My husband has spent his entire career fighting people like that overseas, and he damned sure doesn't want to see it continue here."

Shauna didn't give him time to interrupt and the chief just stood there listening to her story with an emotionless face she couldn't read. She didn't know if he was buying a word of it or not, but she went on, filling in enough details that if he really was a contractor like Eric, he would know that she knew what she was talking about and wasn't simply making stuff up. After telling him the highlights of their journey beginning in the boatyard in Florida, the chief finally stopped her.

"You're either telling the truth or you're really good at spinning fiction on the fly, lady. If it *is* true, then you'll get your chance to tell it to someone in the Army eventually, and maybe they'll look into verifying this Navy SEAL husband of yours. But that's above my pay grade and outside of my area of specialty, so I'll leave it up to the people who do that kind of thing. In the meantime, my mission is clear. I'm here to remove civilians and insurgent elements from the area by whatever means necessary. I have authorization to search and destroy, and with evidence we've found here, I don't have to bother taking you in at all, but I'm going to anyway."

"You can't force me to go anywhere with you. I haven't committed any crime! I was a guest here at this cabin before the owner died, and my husband will be returning here with our daughter when he finds her. He won't know where to look for me if I'm not here!"

"You're right, maybe I can't force you, but I can shoot you if you don't cooperate. I'm giving you a chance because your story may be true, but you'll have to tell it to someone who cares. You can't stay here, because my orders are to destroy any potential insurgent hideouts in these mountains, along with any supplies and equipment found with them. There's no place in this sector that is safe for you, so you'll be better off where you're going. Once we get you back to our operations center, we'll arrange for your transfer into government custody."

"But I already told you what I was doing here! I'm no threat to the government or anyone else. Take all the guns and ammo and whatever else you think you have to confiscate, but please, let me stay here and wait for my husband! We'll leave as soon as he gets back."

"I'm sorry, but I can't do that. Like I said, I can't leave this place standing." With that, he turned back to his man, Jenkins: "Have the men sort all the weapons and ammo and useful supplies and load it onto those horses. Then burn the rest; along with the cabin and barn."

"Why would you burn down this beautiful cabin?" Shauna pleaded. "It was that poor man's dream. He spent years building it!" She was thinking, of course, of Jonathan and Vicky. Wherever they were, she was sure that they would return here soon. She hoped it would be after all of these men were gone, so that they wouldn't be taken prisoner too, but even if they escaped that, they would need the cabin for shelter until they could get somewhere else. It was bad enough that the men were taking all the firearms, supplies and horses. But to burn the cabin too? That was a disaster.

"I already told you. It's part of the job I agreed to. If I leave structures like this standing in these remote areas, they'll be used by the insurgent and terrorist groups that find them. If your husband was the operator you say he was, then he'd tell you the same thing. This is pretty much standard procedure in this type of fluid environment."

"My husband isn't, and *never was* a mercenary at war with law-abiding American citizens! This is a disgrace and goes against everything he stands for, and everything this country stands for!"

"Lady, I don't know whether you know much about what's going on everywhere else or not, but if this situation isn't brought under control, this country isn't going to stand for anything, because it's no longer going to *stand!* You can call me and my men whatever you like if it makes you feel better, but it's people like us who can get the job done. I did my time in this country's military too, and my friends bled and died for what it stands for. Law-abiding citizens aren't my enemy, but lately it's been hard to tell who is and who isn't. The only policy that works is to bring these lawless regions back under control. We're fighting something here that's much bigger than you realize, and it isn't just a bunch of anarchists who don't want to work and pay taxes. Who do you think is instigating all this? Did it occur to you that the money and weapons required to mount such a widespread and effective insurgency is coming from outside the U.S.?

And that this entire mountain region from here to the southern border is wide open to the power-hungry drug cartels that control Mexico? Do you know the extent of what they would do to grab and take over a vast swath of the U.S. while the country is in complete chaos and they think there's no one to stop them? That's why we're clearing these mountains out, because once that's done, we will have a better idea of who the enemy is, and it will pave the way for striking them with decisive action."

Hearing all this, Shauna realized nothing she said was going to change her situation. She would be taken away with these men, and that was that. They could have just as easily killed her as taken her alive, especially since she was armed at the time, giving them ample excuse under their loose rules of engagement, so she had to figure that she was lucky in a way that she would get a chance to plead her case for innocence later. As she stood there thinking of this, she was still afraid that Jonathan and Vicky would show up anytime and be taken into custody with her. She even briefly considered that it might be best for them, since they would all remain together that way and may have a better chance of survival, but Shauna couldn't bring herself to mention them, because she could in no way trust these hired soldiers. Wherever Jonathan and Vicky were at the moment, at least they were free, and though they would be left with no shelter, weapons or supplies, as long as they were free, they would have a shot at survival. Maybe they would even find a way to reunite with Eric, and Megan, if he found her. Shauna could only hope.

She turned away, unable to watch as two of the men set fire to the cabin. She couldn't help but feel that everything that had happened to Bob Barham was her fault. If she hadn't stopped in that one spot along the Divide Trail, Jonathan wouldn't have fallen and broken his leg, and she wouldn't have hiked down this particular drainage and found the cabin. That discovery and the old man's generosity had marked the beginning of the end for him. Now with the cabin and barn gone, and his beloved horses taken away, the only thing remaining of him was his solitary grave at the edge of that lonely high meadow.

Shauna couldn't watch all that go up in flames, but without making it obvious, she was watching the surrounding forest for any sign of Jonathan and Vicky. She couldn't imagine that they had gone far, but they had taken Tucker, the strongest and best trained of the horses they had available, so anything was possible. Shauna could tell that Jonathan had a crush on Vicky almost from the day he met her. She didn't think Vicky felt the same, but there was no way to be sure. It wasn't like they had to leave the cabin to be alone together though, even if that were the reason, unless maybe they were afraid she would return much sooner than expected. Whatever it was that had taken them away, it had saved them for now, and when the other horses were loaded, and the fires were burning with unstoppable fury, the chief ordered his men to move out, and Shauna was led away with them.

They headed back down the drainage in the same direction from which the men had arrived, making Shauna wonder once again if they already knew about the existence of the cabin and had come here specifically to target it. She wasn't going to ask, but she figured that had to be it. If they were indeed working on contract for the military, they probably had access to satellite photos taken before, even if online mapping imagery wasn't available to them now. The cabin would have been visible, and it was likely they were systematically clearing all such remote dwellings if any of what the chief said was the truth.

Bob Barham had told her that the drainage crossed a small gravel road several miles downstream, but Shauna hadn't wandered that far in her hunting and exploration forays from the cabin. Her captors followed the creek all the way down there though, and sure enough, they came to the road Bob described after two or three hours of hiking. Knowing what she knew now of the local area, she wondered if it might be the same road that eventually led up to the site of Vicky's grandparents' ranch, but the contractors weren't going that way. They turned north instead, following the road a short distance before turning off on a narrow, dirt two-track leading out into a flat area of tall pines. Shauna saw why after they'd gone another quarter mile. Hidden there among the trees, were three crew cab pickups and a Land Rover SUV. The men spread out and checked the vehicles, making sure the area was clear before unlocking and starting them. Then, Shauna saw them begin unloading the guns and other supplies from the horses to pile everything into the beds of the pickups. She was shoved into the back seat of the Land Rover, but just before the door was slammed shut, she heard one of the men ask the boss what to do with the horses.

"Shoot them! We can't take them with us."

"NO!" Shauna screamed at him. "Just let them go! They'll be fine on their own!"

The chief came over to the Land Rover and got into the driver's seat. "Until another group of outlaws comes along and uses them to escape justice or attack other citizens. I'm afraid turning them loose is not an option!"

Shauna couldn't look back as two more men climbed into the vehicle with them and the chief pulled away ahead of the trucks. She shuddered when she heard the rifle reports, but she knew it was useless to protest further. How this man could call anyone else an outlaw was beyond her. He was taking the law into his own hands and she found it hard to believe that the U.S. government was paying him to do so. If she ever *did* get a chance to present her side of the story to any real authorities, she wasn't going to leave out what happened here, but she knew even as they drove away that the odds she'd get to tell someone who cared were looking pretty slim.

When they came back out on the main road, the convoy followed the gravel until it ended at a T-intersection with a paved road. From there, they turned west, and Shauna had no idea where they were going; most of the scenery along the way just mile after mile of the same desolate mountain wilderness. At one point they crossed a high pass, winding back and forth up a series of steep switchbacks and then down again in an equally steep descent on the other side. Just to the west of that, the convoy turned off the pavement onto another gravel road, at the end of which was a closed U.S. Forest Service work station that they had apparently converted to their headquarters. The vehicles stopped at the gated entrance to the compound, and the chief chatted briefly with the armed guards there before they proceeded to what appeared to be an equipment building and the chief parked the Land Rover in one of the garage bays. Shauna was then taken to a supply room with a single entrance through a heavy metal door. Once inside, she saw there was just one small window and lots of shelves with boxes of what appeared to be mechanical parts and other related inventory that had probably been there since before the place had been converted over. There was nothing in the room to accommodate an overnight stay; no bathroom, couch or anywhere else to sleep, just a metal desk with an old swivel office chair.

"We don't normally bring guests or prisoners here, so we're not set up for it," the chief explained. "You'll have to sleep on the floor while you're here. Someone will be back with a blanket and a bucket you can use for a toilet. They'll bring you food when we get our evening chow."

With that, the door slammed shut and Shauna heard the sound of a hasp and padlock clicking into place on the outside. There was enough daylight coming through the window for her to see well enough, but the opening section was far too small to accommodate even a slim woman such as herself without breaking out the entire frame, so there was no point in even thinking about trying to escape. Shauna slumped into the office chair as the long and eventful day replayed in her mind. She knew now she should have listened to her gut reaction that day she discovered that Eric had left without them. She should have followed him immediately, insisting that Jonathan and Vicky do the same. Sure, it would have been dangerous, but anything would have been preferable to this. She'd made another mistake by not going with her first instinct, and Shauna spent the rest of the night agonizing over it and wondering if she'd ever see her daughter again. All she knew for sure was that her present situation meant that it was out of her hands for now, and the only thing that gave her a little peace was knowing that at least Eric had a pretty good idea of where Megan went. As long as he got to her and kept her safe, Shauna's main purpose in coming out here was accomplished, even if she never got to share in it. And that was worth dying for if that was the way it had to be.

Six

VICKY HELPED JONATHAN STEADY himself while he dismounted from the saddle and then she took the heavy revolver when he handed it to her. He was about to unbuckle his belt to remove the holster, but she stopped him.

"I don't need it. I'll carry it in my hand and be ready to use it, but don't worry, I won't have to. I know how to move quietly in the woods. Grandpa taught me a lot more than just riding. I'll be careful, and I won't get too close, so they'll never know I'm there. I promise!"

With that, Vicky gave Jonathan a quick hug and left him sitting on a big rock, Tucker's reins in his hands. If he needed to remount the horse on his own, he could stand up on the rock to assist himself. But Vicky didn't plan to let that happen. She knew Jonathan would be helpless out here without her and Shauna, so she couldn't let him down. But at the moment, she was far more worried about Shauna. After finding her rifle destroyed like that, there was little doubt as to whether she'd been taken by those men. And Vicky didn't want to think about what they might do to her. She didn't know what she would be able to do to stop it, but she had to know for sure if they had her and if Shauna was still alive. It was too dangerous to attempt to follow the tracks from where she'd found the rifle, because she had no idea how many more of them might be nearby in the woods or whether or not some were posted along their route, standing guard. She wouldn't be able to see much of the area around the cabin from that approach anyway, so Vicky climbed back up to the crest of the ridge, retracing the route she had taken with Jonathan and Tucker. From up there, she would be able to get a good view, and find out exactly what it was those men intended to do now that they'd discovered the cabin and all the supplies and weapons inside.

Vicky hadn't exaggerated too much when she told Jonathan that she knew how to move quietly in the woods. Although she'd never been interested in hunting and killing animals during her summer visits to her grandpa's ranch, she still loved learning about how the Indians and frontiersmen had survived out there, and the old man had delighted in teaching her what he knew of woodcraft. The main takeaway she got from it was that if one wanted to move unseen and unheard through the woods, the key was to be slow and deliberate about it. She had moved faster when climbing up the backside of the ridge, but once she was descending towards the cabin, Vicky slowed down and paid careful attention to where she put her feet with every step. Although there was a covering of snow, it was still possible to make out the shapes of fallen branches on the ground beneath it with careful scrutiny, so she took the time to avoid accidentally breaking one.

Jonathan had warned her about getting too close, saying the men might begin a sweep of the area at any time. When she finally reached the overlook where the two of them had first observed the men approach the cabin, Vicky saw that she didn't need to get closer to see what she was looking for. *Shauna was there.* She was standing right in front of the cabin with her hands apparently tied behind her back. There were more of the camo-clad men there than she and Jonathan had seen before, some of them standing near Shauna while others moved things out of the cabin and barn. Vicky was relieved and happy to see that Shauna was alive and apparently unhurt, but she was in the hands of those strangers and there was no way of knowing what they were going to do now that they had her.

As she watched them sorting through the rifles and other firearms that had been in the cabin, Vicky could tell that they were questioning Shauna, even though she was much too far away to hear anything that was said. Shauna probably wondered why she and Jonathan weren't there, and Vicky didn't know if the men knew about the two of them or not. She doubted Shauna would tell them anything she didn't have to, but would the men figure it out by looking around in the cabin? Now that they were here, were they planning on taking over the place and staying, waiting them out until Jonathan and Vicky were forced to return that evening because of the cold? Vicky thought they might, until she saw a couple of the men lead the other horses into the barn and then emerge several minutes later with all of them saddled or fitted with Bob's pack saddles. The horses were then led to the pile of stuff in front of the cabin and the men began loading it onto them. *They were taking the horses and all their supplies and firearms with them!* Even if they let Shauna go and left her behind, this was going to put her and Vicky and Jonathan in a desperate situation. But she doubted they would let Shauna go though, and she saw that she was right when some of them began moving back down towards the meadow, leading Shauna and the horses with them. It appeared that they were going back the way they'd came from when Jonathan first spotted them, but three or four of them were still doing something in the cabin and barn as the others waited at the edge of the woods. Vicky knew she had to get back to Jonathan as fast as possible to tell him about Shauna, but she wanted to wait until she knew all of them were gone. When the last of them finally came back out of the cabin and barn, it was only a moment later before Vicky saw smoke—lots of it—and realized what they'd just done. By the time they began disappearing into the woods, the smoke was pouring out of both structures and she caught a glimpse of flames through the open cabin door. Vicky took one last look before turning to hurry back to where she'd left Jonathan. The only good news she had to tell him was that Shauna was alive; for the time being. But they'd lost their shelter, their horses, supplies and weapons, and Jonathan still couldn't walk. She had no idea what they were going to do next.

"Who in the hell are those bastards?" Jonathan fumed when Vicky told him what she'd seen. If they are soldiers, they have no business taking stuff that doesn't belong to them and burning down private property! And they had no reason to take Shauna! What could they possibly accuse her of?"

"Having all those weapons, for one thing. That would be hard to explain. I'm sure she tried, but it must have been no use. But she didn't tell them about us being with her, or else they wouldn't have all left. That tells me she didn't trust them and couldn't convince them of the truth, so they probably aren't soldiers. I'm terrified of what they will do to her, Jonathan!"

"We've got to follow them! We can't let them take Shauna away without knowing where they went, even if there are way too many of them to do anything about it. If we can find out where they're taking her, maybe we can come up with a plan then. Dammit! Maybe Shauna was right! Eric shouldn't have left us here. This wouldn't have happened if we'd all gone with him."

"Now when he comes back, he's going to find us all gone and Bob's place burned to the ground. He'll think we're all dead, even if we aren't!"

"We can't worry about that right now, Vicky. The important thing now is to follow those men. We've got to get going before we lose the trail. There won't be much snow, if any, the farther down that creek they go."

"We can both ride Tucker!" Vicky said. "He won't have any problem carrying the two of us. Come on, I'll help you back up into the saddle and then I'll climb on behind you."

"Maybe for a short distance, but once we pick up their trail, it would probably be best if you walk and lead him by the reins. It'll be easier to move quietly that way, and if they spot us, we'll have a chance to split up and run for it."

Vicky agreed, and once Jonathan was situated in the saddle, she pulled herself up behind him and held on. She knew Jonathan was feeling frustrated and worthless with his bad leg, but with the horse, he had his mobility back, and she was determined to stick with him no matter what. He was a good guy, and he'd come all this way to help people he didn't even know just because Megan's father had befriended him after their chance meeting in Florida. Now Jonathan needed help, and she was all he had. She knew she needed him too, because without him, she would be alone out here again like she was when Eric found her, and that wasn't something Vicky wanted to contemplate even for a moment, so she pushed it out of her mind and reached her arms around Jonathan to take the reins. Jonathan was learning how to handle him, but she and Tucker were old friends and it was best if she were in control now.

Since Vicky had seen the men heading back down the creek when they left the cabin, it seemed probable that they were going back to wherever they came from by the same route that brought them there. She and Jonathan followed the little side creek until they came to the place where it joined the main one, and after a careful pause to look and listen to make sure no one was still in the area, they proceeded on until they found evidence in a patch of snow that the raiding party had indeed passed that way.

"We've got to be careful from here on," Jonathan said. "They could stop almost anywhere, and we could run into them before we realize it."

"You're right. I'll walk from here."

"I'm sorry I can't take a turn at it."

"You're fine, Jonathan. You'll have a better view from up there. Just keep a lookout and keep that rifle handy."

Jonathan did, and Vicky still stopped often to listen, to make sure they weren't following too closely. They didn't see or hear a thing though, but knew they were still on the right trail by the boot prints here and there, many of them pointing downstream, so she pressed on, leading Tucker until the creek came to a place where a gravel road crossed it on a small wooden bridge. There was no snow there, but a quick scan of the sand and mud along the shoulder of the road revealed more tracks, including the hoof prints of horses.

"It looks like they turned right onto this road," Jonathan said.

"If we follow it, we'll be out in the open. I don't like that at all."

"Me either, but I don't see another option. It's the way they went."

The road was indeed the only option, as there was a steep drop-off on one side of it and impenetrable thickets of dense spruce on the other. It would be impossible to follow parallel to it while keeping out of sight, so if they wanted to go the way Shauna had been taken, they had to take the risk of being caught out in the open.

"Let's do it then," Vicky said. "But they may not have stayed on this road for long. We should look for any sign that they turned off again."

"Yeah, that's what I'm thinking too. They probably have a camp set up somewhere nearby since they came to the cabin on foot."

This theory seemed to prove true when they came to a narrow two-track leading off the main road a couple miles to the north. They found tracks indicating that the men had turned that way, but there was something else too.

"Somebody's been driving in and out of here."

"Their camp must be down there for sure then," Jonathan said. "There could be even more of them than the ones we saw."

"There's only one way to find out, but I'm not leading you and Tucker down there."

"It's crazy to go down there at all, Vicky. We know where they are now. We'd better get out of here while we can and try to find Eric."

"We don't really know until one of us sees if there's a camp. Look, it's not as steep here, so I won't use their road. Sneaking down there on foot, I can find a way through the woods. But you and Tucker need to wait over there in those trees and stay out of sight."

"Dammit Vicky, I don't like this one bit!" Jonathan whispered. "If this *is* the entrance to their camp, they've probably got a guard posted, watching this road and all of their perimeter. They may have already seen us, for all we know."

"Then it's too late to worry about it, isn't it? Look, we've got to know where they've taken Shauna, so we can tell Eric if we find him. Just trust me, Jonathan. I'll be all right."

Jonathan wasn't convinced but agreed to wait when she made it clear that she wasn't going to change her mind. Vicky then picked her way through the woods off to one side of the rutted two-track. She didn't have to go far though to discover that it came to an abrupt dead-end. There was no camp, no vehicles and none of the men she'd seen taking Shauna away. But she knew for sure that they'd been here, because the horses they'd taken were all lying dead in the grassy turnabout. Vicky was both heartbroken and furious as she made her way over to them. The animals had all been shot in the head, no doubt simply because those bastards that took them had no more use for them once they got here. The story told by all the tracks in the road was clear now. The men had left their vehicles hidden here when they raided the cabin, and after bringing Shauna and the things they'd taken back with them, they had loaded up and driven away. Vicky knew even as she understood what had happened here that there was no way she and Jonathan could ever hope to find Shauna now. There was no telling how far they would take her, and now that they were in vehicles and on the road, it was impossible to follow their trail. Seeing what they were capable of right here before her eyes, in the senseless slaughter of those innocent animals, Vicky could only fear the worst for Megan's mom. She turned away from the disgusting scene and walked back to where she'd left Jonathan and Tucker.

"That's some sick shit right there, Vicky. It really is! They had no reason to kill those horses. Why didn't they just leave them there and let them fend for themselves if they didn't need them anymore?"

"I don't know, Jonathan. The same reason they burned the cabin and barn, I guess. I don't think those men are soldiers, but I may be wrong. Whoever they are, it doesn't look good for Shauna. What are we going to do, Jonathan? There's no way we'll be able to find her."

"No, you're probably right about that. It sucks, but I don't see how we can help her. We'd better focus on finding Eric, because at least we know where *he* was headed. If we can find him and tell him what happened, maybe he'll have an idea of what to do. We need to try, because there's no sense in him coming all the way back here only to find the cabin gone, especially if he really does find Megan and has her with him."

"What are we going to do about food and shelter though, Jonathan? How are we going to travel that far with only one horse and nothing to eat, not to mention blankets or sleeping bags or anything to help us survive the cold?"

"We'll figure it out, Vicky. While I was waiting on you down there, I just remembered something Bob mentioned one time when he was still at the cabin with me and Shauna. I was in a lot of pain at the time, and probably forgot half of what he said, but he was talking about all his mountain man stuff and how those old-timers used to live up here back in the day. One thing I do remember was that he said something about keeping a cache nearby."

"A cache? Like what?"

"Just a small cache of supplies. He didn't say for sure, but I got the impression he was talking about food. He said the mountain men and prospectors and other folks sometimes did that if they were worried about having to take off in a hurry because of Indian attacks or something."

"Oh wow! That could be good! Do you know where it is?"

"No. At that time I couldn't think about walking or even riding a horse. Bob said he would show me later, when I was able. That's all he said about it, other than that it was at the base of a cliff nearby. He didn't say, but I got the impression it might be in a small cave or something. Don't count on it, Vicky, because it may have just been another one of his stories he made up. The old guy actually thought he *was* a mountain man, I think."

"Well, it's worth looking for anyway."

"Yeah, but first we should go back up to his place and see if there's anything we can salvage from the fire. Maybe everything didn't burn. If we hurry, we can get there before dark. At least we have Tucker, so you won't have to carry me all the way up there on your back," Jonathan grinned.

Returning to the site of the cabin was the place to start, even if this cache Bob had spoken of was a product of his imagination. They might find nothing left there, but at least they'd be back on familiar ground, and it was probably safer there than anywhere else, as it was unlikely those men would return after completing what they came for.

"I'll ride with you on Tucker again if you don't mind being crowded. We won't have to worry as much about being quiet now."

"Sure, I don't mind at all, and I doubt if Tucker does. He's a big, strong horse," Jonathan said.

"Yes, he is, and I am so glad we brought him with us this morning! If we hadn't, he'd be dead like those other poor babies. That just makes me so sad. Why are people so mean?"

"Because they *can* be, Vicky. They don't think they'll have to answer for it now, so they do whatever they want. Killing innocent animals for no reason is about as low as it gets, I guess, and I reckon if they'll do that, they'll do anything."

Vicky knew Jonathan was right, and it sickened her to think of Shauna's fate in the hands of men of that ilk. She and Jonathan would be right there with her if not for the simple fact that he'd wanted to get out of the cabin that morning and work on rehabilitating his leg. But because the two of them had escaped capture, Shauna had one small glimmer of hope, and it was what Jonathan had suggested. They needed to find Eric Branson, and fast, and tell him what happened. From what Jonathan had told her of the man, if anyone could do the impossible, it was Megan's father. He'd been gone far too long for them to ever catch him, but at least they knew where he was headed, and going there to look for him was the only logical thing to do.

It took the rest of the afternoon to make it back to the site of the destruction at Bob Barham's place, and by the time they arrived the sun was going down and the wind was already starting to get chilly. Smoke still rose from both structures, but the flames had mostly burned down, allowing them to approach quite close. The all-wood cabin with its cedar shake roof had been consumed quickly, but there was a pile of rubble remaining that Jonathan said would be worth going through once it had cooled down sufficiently.

"We may be able to salvage some of Bob's tools," Jonathan said. "Maybe an axe head or something useful like that. No chance of any blankets or extra clothing though. It's going to get really cold out here tonight, Vicky. I hope we don't freeze to death!"

Vicky knew Jonathan had little experience with cold weather, especially the extreme cold of high elevations in the Rockies. He was right that it was going to get cold fast, but at this point, it was still survivable, and at least the weather was clear, so they didn't have to worry about a blizzard. "We need to find a place to shelter from the wind, behind a big boulder or something, and then we'll pile up some rocks opposite of it and build a fire. It will reflect some of the heat and make the fire more effective. We can pile up some spruce boughs around us and under us for insulation.

They did all that and it was far better than being out in the open, but whenever they tried to sleep, they soon found themselves shivering each time the fire burned down, and keeping it punched up was going to keep them awake all night.

"We need to get closer," Vicky said.

"If we get any closer to the fire than we already are, we're going to start roasting."

"I don't mean to the fire, Jonathan. I mean to each other. It's a survival technique to prevent hypothermia. Sharing body heat. It's more effective without clothing between the bodies though."

"For real?" Jonathan looked at her with an expression of disbelief.

"Yes, for real! Unless you'd rather sit up all night shivering and putting wood on the fire."

Seven

BEFORE THEY STRIPPED DOWN to their underwear, Vicky made it clear to Jonathan that this was strictly about sharing body heat for the purpose of survival, and that she wasn't interested in fooling around. Jonathan couldn't deny his own interest, but he did his best not to let it show and said nothing, enjoying the close contact with her for what it was, and thankful that she had thought of it. She was certainly right about the effectiveness of the technique. The skin-on-skin contact while wrapped together in their outer garments to keep the warmth in made an amazing difference, maybe even the difference in life and death as the temperatures plummeted during the night. Despite all they'd lost today, they still had each other, and Jonathan felt especially lucky to be stranded there with someone as caring, smart and beautiful as Vicky Singleton. He was learning new things from her every day, and he knew without her help now, he wouldn't survive out here.

Jonathan was warm enough snuggled there with Vicky, but he still had a hard time falling asleep, even after she dozed off. He couldn't stop thinking about what Shauna might be going through that night and it was agonizing knowing he was powerless to help her. Jonathan had developed a lot of respect for that woman over the past several weeks, especially after the two of them had to make their way out here alone when Eric didn't return from his mission for Lieutenant Holton. It sucked that she hadn't been able to evade those men today like he and Vicky had, and Jonathan felt terrible that he hadn't been there with her to try and intervene when it happened. Shauna was a fighter and had already saved his butt when they were attacked on the way into Boulder while riding the bicycles. It made him feel like crap that he couldn't do the same for her and thinking about all that kept him awake for hours. He and Vicky would go and find Eric, but Jonathan didn't have a lot of hope that it would do Shauna much good. A lot of time could pass before Eric found her, if he ever did.

Jonathan finally fell asleep sometime in the early morning hours, but it seemed like only minutes before he woke up shivering again. When he opened his eyes, he saw why. Vicky was no longer close against him, but was up and gathering more wood for the fire that she'd already punched up from last night's coals. It was daylight, but the sun hadn't cleared the ridge to the east of them yet and wouldn't for another hour. Jonathan pulled his clothes and jacket back on and warmed his hands near the fire.

"Did you finally get some sleep?" Vicky asked.

"Yeah, not much, but some. I'm sorry if I kept you awake."

"You didn't. I had a hard time sleeping too, but at least we didn't freeze to death."

"Thanks to you we didn't!"

"That wasn't so bad, was it?"

"Sleeping nearly naked with you? Heck no, it wasn't!"

She blushed and then smiled. "It could have been a lot worse if you were stuck out here with Eric instead, huh?"

"We'd probably both just have to freeze to death in that case."

"It's amazing what a difference one day can make isn't it?" Vicky was staring over at the site of the cabin now, reduced to a pile of blackened rubble. "Yesterday we woke up in a cozy warm cabin, making coffee and breakfast on a wood stove. Now, all we have is the clothes on our backs, and no breakfast, and no coffee."

"Now that you mention it, yeah, I'm pretty hungry. And you don't want to know what I'd do for a hot cup of coffee. No telling when we'll get *that* again. Dang, I wish you hadn't reminded me!"

"Sorry! Hey, before we get any hungrier, we'd better get to looking for that cache you were talking about. If it is real, it might take a while to find it."

"Yeah, and if it isn't, then we'd better find something to shoot pretty fast. We won't last long up here without food, especially as cold as it is."

"Bob said it was at the base of a cliff? Did he say which direction it was from here?"

"No, he didn't go into any details because he said he was going to show it to me himself. I was in no shape to go there with him though before he left with Shauna to go to the ranch, so he never got the chance. You've explored some around here with her though. Have you seen any cliffs that might be the one?"

"That's just it. I really haven't. There's plenty of steep slopes around here, but not an actual cliff that I know of. I'm trying to think of where one might be. Looking at the way that drainage runs, it's bound to be somewhere off to one side of that, but we don't even know if it was upstream or down from here."

"Well, we didn't see anything like that yesterday, and we went all the way down to that road and back. Maybe it's upstream, somewhere between here and up on the Divide Trail."

"That's what I'm thinking, and I believe that's where we ought to start looking."

Once Tucker was saddled up, Jonathan mounted him with Vicky's help and they headed up the steep slopes of the drainage towards the Continental Divide. The springs feeding the creek were only a short distance up, and beyond them the basin widened, and it was in that area that it seemed more likely they would find this "cliff" that Bob spoke of. They explored several frustrating dead ends, but it wasn't until they were almost up to the saddle of the ridge, near the place where Jonathan broke his leg, that Vicky spotted something high up on a steep slope to the south that looked promising. It was more of a small rock wall than a "cliff," but it was the closest they'd seen to one, and it seemed to overhang beyond vertical, indicating there could be a cave at the base.

"Tucker can't get up there, so you're going to have to wait here," Vicky said.

"Yeah, yeah. I know the drill. Just be careful, okay? Take the .44 Magnum with you and if there *is* a cave, make sure it's not a bear or mountain lion den!"

"Not likely, but I'll make sure nothing's home before I go in."

Jonathan didn't like the idea of poking around in caves out here himself. It would really suck to crawl into one and corner a big pissed-off animal like that. Thinking about it reminded him how lucky he was to have Vicky and Tucker. He figured if he'd been left alone out here in the shape he was in, it would just be a matter of time before something came stalking out of the woods and made a meal out of him. Predators always preferred weak or crippled prey, given a choice, and he figured being eaten alive would be about the worst way to go he could imagine. It made him so nervous thinking about it that he wanted to call out to Vicky to make sure she was still okay. She was out of sight from where he waited, but they were also close enough to that trail up on the ridge above that he didn't want to risk it. There was no way of knowing who might be passing through the area, and keeping a low profile was essential. But she was gone so long that he was almost ready to break that rule when he finally spotted her coming back down. Vicky was carrying something balanced across her shoulder that looked like a wool blanket, tied up into a bundle. In her free hand, she was carrying a short rifle.

"I hit the jackpot! Old Bob wasn't just telling a tall tale, Jonathan! I found his cache!"

"No shit? What was in it?"

"Food, like you said! And check out this rifle! It's a .22 Magnum, like the varmint gun my grandpa had! There were two 50-round boxes of cartridges for it. There was also a nice hunting knife, a compass, a map and a couple of pencils, a box of waterproof matches and this blanket. We'll be warmer at night wrapped up in this, Jonathan!"

"You'll share it with me? Do we still get to take our clothes off?"

"That depends on whether you behave," she laughed.

"I will! But right now, I'm starving! What is there to eat?"

Vicky put down her load and untied the blanket. Jonathan grinned when he saw what old Bob Barham had stashed in there. It was certainly an emergency survival cache, stocked with high-energy rations that included freeze-dried backpacker meals, high energy bars, and vacuum-packed jerky that he'd probably made himself. It wasn't a huge amount, but used carefully, there was enough to see him and Vicky through a few days, and the .22 Magnum carbine would be ideal for hunting smaller game to supplement it if needed.

"This is awesome, Vicky! Did you get everything he had in there?"

"I think so. It was dark, of course, and the cave was really small. He'd piled rocks and brush in front of it to hide it, so that's what took me so long. It was just big enough for a person to crawl inside and I had to feel my way around."

"No freakin' way I'd do something like that! You're a lot braver than I am, Vicky!"

"Well I knew a lion or bear couldn't have gotten in there the way he had it closed off, and it's too high and cold up here for rattlesnakes, so what was there to worry about? It paid off, right?"

Jonathan gave her a big hug and told her it sure did. Then they opened a couple of the energy bars and shared them before heading back down to the cabin. There were two things Jonathan wanted to do there; one was to look through the cabin rubble for anything else they might need, and the other, now that they had something to write with, was to leave Eric a note somewhere that he'd find it. It was as likely he'd arrive here first as it was they'd find him—probably more so, actually—and Jonathan wanted him to know what happened to Shauna and where the two of them had gone.

They left the note at the base of the marker Eric had erected for Bob Barham's grave. Vicky had the better handwriting, so she wrote it on the back of part of the map that had been in Bob's cache. The map itself was a national forest map showing hundreds of thousands of acres of the surrounding federal lands. After looking it over they tore off a section that they knew was far from their route and therefore unneeded, and it was big enough to write a detailed note. Vicky worded it so that if the men that had done this or anyone else with bad intent found it, they wouldn't be able to make sense of where the two of them were headed, but Eric would know. She also described the location of the place they'd followed the trail of the raiders to, which was Shauna's last known location. If the same men came back and read that, they would know they'd been followed, but Jonathan and Vicky thought that was unlikely anyway and that it wouldn't make a difference if they did. But if Eric read it, that location would be crucial information to him, even though they doubted he would be able to follow the trail from that point any better than they could have. It was going to be heartbreaking for Eric if he had indeed found Megan and returned here only to discover her mother had been abducted in the meantime. But they left him as much information as they could and that was all Jonathan and Vicky could do unless they found him first, either at the reservation or somewhere along the way back from there.

They carefully wrapped the note in one of the plastic bags Bob had used for the food in the cache, and then covered it under a small cairn of rocks, leaving just enough of the bag showing to let Eric know something was in there if he walked over to the grave site. Then, the two of them used sticks to sift through the rubble of the cabin. There were some metal tools and a few other objects that didn't burn, but they never found an axe head or anything else worth salvaging that they could carry, and so they loaded up what they had from the cache behind the saddle on Tucker's back and set out on their journey. Neither of them wanted to spend another night in the vicinity of the cabin, even if they didn't have time to get far with what was left of the afternoon, so they headed back up the creek and stopped for the night near the place where Vicky had found the cave. Once there, they built a fire, so they could heat water for one of the freeze-dried meals. That second night was far more comfortable than the one before, as they didn't have to try and fall asleep on empty stomachs, and they now had a blanket they could share. Sleeping close for warmth wasn't quite as awkward this second time either, and they fell naturally into each other's arms with little hesitation.

"I feel a lot better about our chances of making it now, Jonathan, thanks to Bob for leaving us what we needed."

"He was prepared for everything, wasn't he? He was such an interesting and knowledgeable man. It's really too bad what happened to him. We could have learned a lot from the guy."

"Yeah, if not for that stupid Jeremy and Brett."

"I still think Eric went too easy on them, letting them go. He probably should have shot them then and there."

"Probably, but of course when confronted they dropped their guns and played it off as an accident, whether it really was or not. I don't see Eric as the kind of guy who would just shoot someone under circumstances like that."

"No, I just wish the idiots would have tried something with him. He wouldn't have hesitated to blow them away then."

"Well, like he said, he didn't do them any great favors letting them go the way he did. With no horses, no guns and barely enough food to get them down out of the mountains, I don't imagine they had an easy time of it. And they may not have survived it after all."

"Maybe not. It just sucks that Bob had to go that way. But a lot of bad things are happening to a lot of good people; like your grandparents, and now Shauna. Sometimes I wonder if any of us are going to make it through this, and if life will ever be normal again. I doubt it will. I really do."

"It may not ever return to normal, Jonathan, but while we are alive, we can make the best of it."

"I'm not complaining about that. I know we're lucky to be alive, and I'm especially lucky to have you for a friend. Otherwise, it would be over for me out here."

"And I'm just as lucky, Jonathan. I can't tell you how awful it was for me those days and nights when I was alone hiding in that barn at the ranch, after having to bury my grandma and grandpa by myself. I don't ever want to feel that alone again. It was horrible!"

Vicky snuggled closer to him as she said this, and Jonathan hugged her tightly, promising her that wouldn't happen again. "We'll stick together, Vicky, whatever comes next. I know Eric wants to get the hell out of the country and he's got a great boat to do it on. He won't leave without Megan, and I know he'll do everything in his power to find Shauna too, if she's still alive. But at some point, he's going to be setting sail again, and if he'll let me, I want to go with him. You ought to think about that too. From what I've seen since we left Florida, I don't know if this country will ever be the same again."

"Where is he planning to go? I never thought about the idea of leaving on a sailboat, but then, I've lived in the mountains most of my life."

"Eric's been all over the world in his line of work. He knows where all the bad places are and where to find the good ones too. He told me all about some of them when we were sailing across the Gulf. Whole groups of islands so far away from everything else that hardly anybody ever goes to them except a few other people with the kind of sailboats that can get there. He said there were places where you could anchor up for years if you wanted to, with coral reefs full of fish and perfect weather year-round. Wouldn't it be nice to be soaking up rays on a tropical beach somewhere under the full moon instead of freezing our asses off up here? Think about it!"

"It does sound nice, Jonathan, and maybe I'll dream about it when I fall asleep, at least as long as you stay close enough to keep me warm."

Jonathan pulled her even closer to him with that and said he would dream of it too. And they soon fell asleep in each other's arms, but when he woke it was to a bitter north wind sweeping down over the divide, shattering any dreams of tropical paradise against the harsh reality of their situation. Jonathan built up the fire for Vicky this time, and then they shared another quick meal and moved out.

"We're going to have to find a campsite at lower elevations tonight," Vicky said. "It feels like a front coming through, and I'll bet we're going to see some snow. We need to find an alternate route that doesn't follow the divide too.

That trail's going to keep us too high for this weather. It's way too late in the year for that already."

Jonathan trusted that Vicky knew what she was talking about. They were faced with either taking their chances being seen by the wrong people while traveling the trails and roads of the valleys, or the prospect of dying of exposure in the high country. It wasn't a difficult choice because freezing was certain if they stayed up there. They had to keep pushing south, and the only way to do that was to leave the divide and work their way through the mountains to one side. The map Bob had left showed a network of trails in the vicinity, and where they connected to what few gravel and paved roads there were. But the map was limited to just the national forest they were presently within.

By the end of their third full day of travel, they had left the boundaries of that forest and were traveling by compass and guesswork, keeping to the trails and remote roads that led in the general direction they wanted to go. Twice when on such a road, they heard the approach of vehicles and had to quickly move into the brush to hide and wait for them to pass. On both occasions, the vehicles were running in company with others; the first a group of three pickup trucks, two of them pulling horse trailers behind them, and the second, a small convoy of SUVs following each other closely. They managed to stay out of sight both times, but close encounters like that made Jonathan nervous, and where the terrain permitted, they avoided using such roads and instead cut cross country.

This lower elevation route put them in proximity to ranches and isolated houses, but most seemed abandoned, and some were burned to the ground the same as Bob Barham's cabin. Jonathan and Vicky took turns studying the intact ones carefully from a distance with the scope Jonathan took off of Shauna's ruined rifle, but they saw no signs of life other than the vehicles that had passed. People apparently had either left on their own, or perhaps been killed or taken away like Shauna. Although he and Vicky figured some of those homes remaining might contain items they could use, they didn't dare risk approaching them for fear someone might still be hiding out there that would shoot them on sight. It was far safer to make do with what they had, and so that was what they did.

Once they were a considerable distance from the last ranch they'd seen, and sunset was rapidly approaching, Jonathan had the opportunity to put the .22 Magnum rifle to use when he and Vicky flushed a rabbit that stopped after running just a few feet, presenting an easy target. He was pleased with his luck and told Vicky it was time to start thinking about hunting more, as they had no idea how long it was going to take to reach the Jicarilla reservation. When they were discussing the trip with Eric before he cut out on all of them, he'd estimated it would take about a week by way of the Continental Divide Trail. They had studied the maps enough that Jonathan and Vicky both had some idea of how to find the place once they reached New Mexico, but the circuitous route they were forced to take now would no doubt add days of travel time.

They camped near the place where Jonathan killed the rabbit, in a sheltered creek bottom among a stand of towering pines. Then, Jonathan dressed it while Vicky built the cooking fire, and by the time they were eating, it was fully dark, and everything changed. The first indication they had that they weren't alone was when Tucker became agitated. He had smelled or heard something out there beyond the circle of light cast by the flames, and then when Jonathan and Vicky heard the loud crack of a breaking branch, they knew someone, or something had stepped on it.

"It could be a bear!" Jonathan whispered, as he moved to reach for the .45-70 carbine. But before he laid a hand on it, a sharp voice from out of the dark stopped him short:

"Don't touch that rifle! Put your hands up; high, where I can see them, and stay where you are! Both of you!"

Eight

FOR ERIC BRANSON, THE drive across the Jicarilla reservation in the battered old Toyota pickup bordered on surreal. Less than an hour ago, he'd been alone in the jail cell where he'd been held since his arrival, expecting yet another interrogation or worse when his Apache guards came to unlock him. Nothing could have prepared him for what happened next though, when he was led down a hall and through the doors of the tribal headquarters office. After all he'd been through and all the miles he'd traveled in search of his daughter, Megan was sitting right there in front of him! And now he was squeezed into the compact cab of the little truck next to her, as she sat in the middle between him and her friend, Aaron, who was at the wheel. Ahead of them on the dusty gravel road was Aaron's uncle and aunt, leading the way back to their place where Megan had been staying since her arrival here.

Eric knew that Megan was beyond happy as she sat there between the two of them. She certainly hadn't been expecting to see her dad here, and she'd been worried sick over her friend Aaron ever since she'd seen him abducted by the armed men who'd taken him away to their camp. When Eric told her he'd found that camp destroyed and littered with bodies, Megan had naturally feared the worst. Seeing Aaron suddenly drive up to the tribal headquarters in that old truck, alive and well, was almost too good to be true. Eric could tell it was the best day his daughter had seen in a long time, even though some of the things he told her during the drive no doubt brought back unpleasant memories from her recent past.

"Vicky's grandparents were so sweet, and so good to us. They didn't deserve to die like that. I can't imagine what Vicky must have gone through, being all alone there after it happened. If we'd known that was going to happen, we'd have never left."

"It probably wouldn't have made a difference," Eric said, "other than it may have gotten you both killed. You made the right choice to get away from Gareth and his friends."

"I can't believe he had the nerve to go back there, after all he stole from the ranch. And now he's dead. I suppose it was bound to happen. Gareth couldn't be content to just focus on survival, like the rest of us were doing. He was always looking for something more."

"Yep, it sure seems that way to me, from what I've heard about him," Eric said.

"I was a fool to ever listen to anything he said in the first place. I'm sorry, Dad. I'm sorry I caused you all that trouble without even knowing it."

"You have nothing to apologize for and nothing to regret, Megan. We all make mistakes. The best you can do is learn from them." Eric knew that Megan had been infatuated with Gareth, and maybe even thought she was in love with him before she found out who he really was. But hearing of his demise now, she didn't exhibit any emotion to indicate that she still clung to even a shred of those feelings. Relief was all he sensed from her, and understandably so.

Her friend Aaron had been listening to the conversation without comment as he drove, but when Megan said nothing else about Gareth, he questioned Eric's other actions at the ranch.

"So, you just let Brett and Jeremy go free? Even after they killed that old man you were riding with?"

"I did. But only because I don't think Jeremy meant to kill him. It was a mistake and Bob *did* have a gun in his hand. I know they were in with Gareth and with him when he tried to track the two of you down, but you know as well as I do that letting them go with no supplies or weapons wasn't exactly doing them any favors. They really only had one option if they wanted to survive, and that was to head down out of the high country and try to find their way to one of the refugee camps. I have no idea whether they made it or not, but it's not my problem and I haven't given it any more thought."

"You did the right thing, Dad. They did some stupid things, but it was Gareth that influenced them. He had a way about him that made people want to follow him, but the more that happened, the more he started changing. He went off the deep end pretty quickly, and I'm glad he won't be hurting anyone else."

"No, he won't. You don't have to worry about that."

"No, but now I've got to worry about Mom! I can hardly believe she came all this way with you! That's insane!"

"I don't think it's insane at all Megan. She *is* your mom, you know, and you know how tough your mom is. She's not afraid of anything. She would have eventually made her way out here to find you with or without me."

"I'm sorry I put you both through all that worry. I should have tried to get home as soon as the semester was over, before things started getting bad. It's just that no one thought it was going to get *this* bad."

"You made the best decision at the time, Megan, given the information you had. You were a lot better off staying put than going back to Florida, considering the impact of that hurricane."

"So, our house is like totally destroyed, huh?

"Not leveled like some, but yeah, that whole area is uninhabitable now, and will be for the foreseeable future, because nobody's there to restore services."

"That's really sad. I feel so bad for all my friends and the other people I know down there. I hope they made it somewhere safe and somehow survived. I feel bad for Andrew and my stepdad too. I know it must be hard on them, losing everything and having to leave it all behind."

"They'll be okay. They're with your Uncle Keith and your Grandpa, so they're as safe as they could be anywhere right now."

"That's awesome that all of you sailed all the way to Uncle Keith's from Florida!"

"Daniel wasn't too happy about the idea at first, but he came around."

"And he was cool with my mom taking off out here alone with you?"

"I wouldn't say he was exactly *cool* with it, but he managed to deal with it. It's not like he had a choice. Your mom wasn't having any part of staying behind, and there was no way I was bringing him and Andrew with us."

"I can see that. They wouldn't have been able to handle all you've been through to get here."

"Not likely. The way it turned out though, your mom and I didn't end up traveling together most of the time anyway."

"And now you've left her waiting again," Megan said. "I can't imagine that she's happy with you about that. I can just hear her now, the day she woke up and discovered that you left without telling her."

"I'm sure she had a few choice names for me, especially after she read my letter, but it couldn't be helped. I didn't want anyone slowing me down once I knew where you were headed. They are safe where I left them, and they have everything they need right there in that cabin. The only problem is that now I have to go back there to get them."

"Not by yourself though, right? You know I'm going with you."

Eric hadn't thought that far ahead yet at all. Until that afternoon, his entire focus and mission in life was finding Megan. He'd vowed to turn over every rock in these mountains to find her, if that's what it took, and he'd fought his way through a world of shit to get here. But now that he'd found her alive and unhurt, he needed to make plans for the next phase. Getting Shauna, Jonathan and Vicky was a top priority, but he wasn't ready to commit to taking Megan with him just yet, at least not until he had a better understanding of the situation here on the reservation, so he could assess whether or not it was safe to leave her here.

"If you go, I'm going with you," Aaron said to Megan, before turning to Eric: "My uncle and my other relatives will help us too, Mr. Branson. They will provide horses, supplies, weapons, whatever we need…"

"We'll talk about that later," Eric said. Despite his run-in with the militia forces in the mountains and getting thrown in jail by the tribal police here on Jicarilla land, finding Megan hadn't taken as long as Eric had expected when he left Shauna and the others behind. The three of them were well-supplied at the cabin, with plenty of food, firewood and other necessities, so it wasn't like he had to leave today to rush back after them. There was still a lot to talk to Megan about, and many questions to ask her about all she'd been through in these months that changed her life from a carefree college student to a refugee of war in her own country. There was no need to burst her bubble now, but Eric doubted he'd be taking her and Aaron with him when he went back to that cabin. As much as he hated the thought of letting her out of his sight again, it didn't make sense to expose her to more danger than necessary. It was going to be tough and risky enough getting all of them back to Louisiana, and Eric still had no idea how he was going to go about doing that. It was a bridge to be crossed when the time came, but for now he was content to be sitting there with his arm around Megan's shoulders, knowing she was alive and unhurt.

Eric had never given up on Megan, despite what he'd found since arriving at the campus in Boulder. His girl was a survivor, and she'd proven it, no doubt aided by some of the things he'd taught her long ago during what little time he'd had with her between overseas deployments. She'd also gotten a lot of help from her friends, including Vicky and her deceased grandparents, and the brave young man beside her who'd been willing to bring her here to his homeland despite the risks of the journey. Eric was looking forward to talking more with the young Apache man, who clearly knew his way around in the mountains and deserts of his ancestral homeland. He owed the boy his gratitude for what he'd done for Megan, and he looked forward to meeting more of his people now that he was no longer considered a trespasser, but rather a guest. Eric didn't have hard feelings towards the men of the security patrol despite his treatment. He knew all too well how a lack of communication between different branches of an organization could lead to such circumstances. Fortunately, someone from the reservation had finally put two and two together and remembered the young white woman who had recently arrived seeking refuge and claiming to be a friend of Aaron Santos. The charges against him were dropped of course, as soon as Megan identified him when the jailor brought him to the council room. It was only after they arrived at the home of Aaron's Uncle Ethan and Aunt Ava that Eric learned why the security detail had been so persistent in tracking and apprehending him once he entered Jicarilla land.

"Those people are taking control of as much land as they can, especially the remote areas that are uninhabited or only have a few isolated ranches here and there," Ethan told Eric. "Our lands are directly along the corridor they are using between Mexico and the north, and so they have been crossing our borders as well. They think they can intimidate people and drive them out, but it will never work with us."

"Who?" Eric asked. "Who is doing this?"

"The drug cartels from Mexico, and their hired soldiers on both sides of the border. They are more powerful than ever now, and they are using the breakdown of law and order as an opportunity to move north and take over the entire region."

Eric remembered Keith mentioning rumors of this happening in the west, and he'd heard bits and pieces from others over the course of his journey here as well. If this was true, it would better explain the presence of the 'militia' groups he'd encountered in the mountains, but with the economy in shambles and most people in survival mode, Eric had to wonder what kind of market there would be for the illicit products of the cartels.

"It's not just about money," Ethan explained. "The biggest cartels have more money than some entire small countries. They are after power and control, because they know that eventually the market will be back. They are looking to expand their bases and eliminate their competition.

The border has always been a problem, even though it never did much to stop their business. But now what is going on everywhere is making things so much easier for them. They are counting on the anarchy that's happening across the country to result in its collapse. And since little has been done to stop them, they are taking what they want and killing anyone who gets in their way."

Ethan couldn't give him more details than that, and Eric still had to wonder how much of what the old man was telling him was truth and how much was rumor. He could see that it was plausible, and it made him curious for sure, because he definitely wanted to avoid crossing paths with these cartels when he headed back east with his family.

"You can get a lot more information from Nantan and some of the other fellows in the tribal security force. They have been watching not only our reservation borders, but the passes and other natural routes beyond them, and they have seen some of the activity I'm talking about. They will be glad to talk to you now that they know who you are, and that you are not working for those criminals. Your daughter tells me that you are a soldier yourself, and that you've seen plenty of action, probably worse than anything here."

"I've seen a lot, but now that I've been back a while, I'm not sure it was any worse," Eric said. "This is a crazy situation our country is in."

"And it will probably get more so, from what we've heard. Our people don't want any part of it unless they bring it to us. But we intend to keep our homelands and if anyone tries to take them from us, we will fight. It won't be the first time the Apache fought for these lands, and we will honor the sacrifices of our ancestors with our own blood if necessary. This land is all we have left now, and here, we will stand our ground."

Eric nodded. Aaron's uncle was probably in his sixties, but he was hard and lean from a lifetime of working outdoors, and he reminded Eric of his own father, Bart. Eric had no doubt Ethan would indeed fight to defend his homeland. It wasn't Eric's fight, but the information the man had given him was something that he certainly wanted to follow up on. He would meet with those tribal security guys before he finalized his plans to go back north to the cabin. Any intel they could give him on the movements of these cartels would be useful in planning his route so as to avoid them.

"I'm sure Aaron won't mind driving you back to town tomorrow," Megan said when Eric told her what he had in mind that evening after dinner, while the two of them took a short walk near the ranch house.

"Aaron seems like a good guy, and a smart one too, I suppose, considering he talked you into coming here."

"He *is* a good guy, Dad! I didn't really get to know him until we all left the campus together to hike to that ranch. I was so wrapped up in Gareth at the time, I just didn't notice. I was totally being stupid!"

"You weren't stupid, Megan, probably just infatuated. But you got your butt out of Boulder, and that's what's important. It wasn't looking good there at all by the time I arrived. The campus has been converted into essentially a detention center. You'd be locked up there if you'd stayed and were lucky enough to survive."

"What's going to happen to all those people they're keeping like that, Dad? They can't hold them indefinitely, can they?"

"I honestly don't know, Megan. The rules have changed, and whoever is in control can do whatever they want, I suppose. It's a really bad situation, far worse than the rumors I'd heard, and I'd already heard enough to know that I had to come back here and get you and your mom out. And your grandpa and uncle. It's too bad your Aunt Lynn didn't make it, but nothing can be done about that now. The main thing is to get you and your mom back to Louisiana, so we can all get on the boat and leave this mess behind us."

"That seems pretty extreme to me, Dad. Does it really make sense to leave the whole country? All we need to do is stay away from the main roads and towns, right? I mean, it seems safe enough right here to me. Aaron said so."

"Aaron just got here too. He probably hasn't heard everything his Uncle Ethan just told me. They aren't immune to trouble here just because this is reservation land. The troublemakers aren't respecting any boundaries, not even national ones. Remote doesn't necessarily make you safe either. That ranch you and Aaron left was remote too, but now the house is burned to the ground and Vicky's grandparents are buried there. Your mom and Vicky and my friend, Jonathan could be in danger too, even as remote as that cabin is, so I don't plan to delay returning there to get them out."

"What is Vicky going to do? She doesn't have any place to go with her grandparents dead and her mom living so far away. I can't just leave her here alone. I mean, I'm sure Aaron and his aunt and uncle wouldn't mind, but I was hoping we could all stick together. Maybe we should wait here for a little while and see. Besides, how would we get to Louisiana anyway?"

"We'll figure all that out when the time comes, Megan. Just try not to worry about it right now. The main thing I have to do is go to that cabin and get them. Let's take this one step at a time. It always works best that way, right?"

"Yeah, you always say that. I'm sorry. I just can't help thinking ahead too though."

"You've done a great job so far, Megan. I knew you were a survivor, and I knew you wouldn't just sit around that campus waiting to see what was going to happen. Now we've got to work together as a team again to get through what's next."

"That's why I need to go with you. Me and Aaron both want to go. If we're a team, then we should stick together. It doesn't make sense for us to just sit here. If something happens and you don't make it there, we'd never know. Just like Mom and Vicky and Jonathan don't know that you've found me yet. If you hadn't left them there, we'd all be together now."

"I did what I thought was best, Megan. I couldn't afford to wait, and I didn't know what I'd run into out there. Sometimes you just have to make decisions and go with them."

"Then let me make mine! My decision is to go back there with you, and with Aaron."

"We'll talk about it tomorrow, Megan. First, I plan to meet with those tribal security guys that arrested me, and now that we're on better terms, see what intel I can get from them before I plan my route."

Nine

"SO, WE MEET AGAIN; the mysterious white man caught sneaking onto Apache lands! I apologize for the rough treatment, but it didn't look too good, the way you arrived."

"My bad," Eric said, after shaking hands with Nantan, the tribal council member who'd also been leading the security team that apprehended him for trespassing that first morning he'd arrived here. "I guess I've gotten used to using the back door and not knocking first. It's been necessary in most of the places I've worked lately."

"So I've heard. I understand that you were a special forces operator; a Navy SEAL, no less."

"In another lifetime, or so it seems now." Eric said.

"Marine Recon myself. I've played in some of the world's hotspots too. As have several of my brothers here on the reservation."

"Well, I can see that you're keeping in good practice and running top-notch security. Thanks for taking me alive for questioning. I guess it could have gone differently, and you would have been within your rights."

"You seemed a little too interesting to shoot on the spot. It took some balls to come in here alone, and we wanted to hear your story... who you were working for... and why they sent you... Some of the guys wanted to use the old methods of my people to make you sing, considering they caught you sneaking onto our land like an enemy, but I could tell you were a warrior, and I knew you were a worthy adversary, even if you didn't really have a chance."

"I've heard the Apache could be quite creative with their enemies back in the day, and with good reason, considering how many your ancestors had. This is a beautiful piece of land you have here. I don't blame you for wanting to keep it that way."

"It's barely a fragment of what my people once had, but you know that story and that's a topic for another time. We aren't trying to take anything back though, and the purpose of our security is not to quarrel with the government. Like I said, most of us served that same government, fighting America's enemies overseas. But you know how thin military resources are spread all over the world now. And with what's happening here at home, they can barely contain the problems even in the populated areas of the cities and coasts. They're not even in control of the border out here in the west. Maybe in some places down in Texas, but certainly not in Arizona and New Mexico. And they sure aren't concerned with the mountains and deserts up here, far away from everything and barely populated to begin with. And that is the problem. It leaves huge areas free for the taking by whoever has the most guns."

Eric said that Ethan had told him as much, and then he told Nantan what he had seen in the mountains to the north, how he'd encountered the small militia camp first, then found the much larger one that had been wiped out.

"That was a military strike," he said. "Aaron can attest to it, because he was being held there when it happened, along with others who'd been caught crossing the militia-held wilderness area there. My own daughter barely avoided capture, and then found her way to an Army checkpoint on the highway east of those mountains. I'm pretty sure it was her report that led to the execution of the strike."

"Maybe," Nantan said. "But there is heavy fighting going on between these groups that would surprise you. Some of them are far more organized than you would think, and they are well-funded. Many of the soldiers they have working for them are professional mercenaries from all over the world. The cartels are throwing everything they have at expanding their business while they have this window of opportunity. They are collaborating with and supplying weapons to the jihadists and anyone else who will help them create more chaos and kill more of their opposition. So, it is difficult to know who the enemy is and where they will strike next. But we are interested in everything you have seen, as we are trying to gather all the intel we can about the lands surrounding our reservation and beyond."

"Understood," Eric said, "and I'm trying to learn more likewise. As you already know by now, I have to go back there, through that same area to get my ex-wife and two friends. I was hoping you and some of your men who know the area could help me choose the best route to make the quickest trip. It seems that horses are the best option, and I have the two I came here with, but I want to take a couple more just in case. And I'll need supplies. I can pay you well for any of this you can spare."

"We won't sell you horses, but your daughter is a friend of one of ours, and you are a brother in arms who has fought in the same wars we have. Like us, you are looking after your own people now, and like our people, your family is threatened by the same enemies that threaten us. You won't have to go alone, because we will help you bring your friends and the mother of your daughter back. Those of us who go with you will do so not only to help you though, but because we want to see for ourselves the extent of these operations that threaten our lands."

Eric wasn't expecting this at all. These same men who'd beaten and interrogated him now regarded him as a friend and even a brother. "That's a generous offer, Nantan, but aren't you worried about dividing your forces, and leaving your lands more vulnerable to encroachment while you're away?"

"That is something to consider, but no, I'm not worried. We won't be gone all that long, and the men of our security forces have the advantage of knowing every detail of the land here and the nearby lands beyond our borders. It only takes a few scouts to keep tabs on the movements of anyone trespassing nearby. But if some of us go and learn more of where those people are basing their operations, then perhaps we can take the fight to them before they bring it here. Generations may have passed, but it's not too late to learn from the tactics of our war chiefs, who were very good at defeating many, even when their numbers were few."

Eric couldn't argue with that. He knew enough history to know the difficulty the U.S. Army had in subduing the last defiant Apaches of the late 1800's. Those hardy warriors were masters of guerrilla warfare and of using their knowledge of the harsh landscape they inhabited to their advantage against what would seem impossible odds. What the Army learned during the course of the Apache Wars eventually contributed to the training Eric and other special forces operatives like him had received. And using disloyal indigenous scouts to hunt down notorious and elusive warlords worked as well in Afghanistan as it eventually had with Geronimo.

It would be good to have the company of fellow warriors who knew the territory for his trip back to the cabin, but Eric knew too that it might come with a price. It sounded to him like Nantan and some of his buddies were ready to go on the warpath, and Eric didn't really want to get involved in any fighting if he didn't have to, but then again, everything was a tradeoff. It would likely take longer if he went alone, because he would be relying on the trails and main roads he'd used to get here, not knowing the shortcuts these guys could show him. And while he didn't feel that he needed backup on the way out, it would be nice to have some extra guns for the journey back, when he wouldn't be looking out for himself alone. He knew Shauna could pull her weight, but he was unsure about Vicky, and with that broken leg still in the healing process, Jonathan wasn't going to be a hundred percent for at least a few more weeks.

"Only a few of us will go, maybe four or five, if you agree to this." Nantan said. "I will be one, and we will finalize the rest after a brief meeting and discussion."

"I'm fine with it, if you're sure you really want to go to all that trouble," Eric said. "But how soon can you leave? I am anxious to get started because the weather in the mountains is only going to get worse, and I've already left them alone there in that cabin long enough. They are bound to be getting anxious by now, and knowing my ex-wife like I do, I'm not sure how long her patience is going to last before she decides to head this way on her own."

"We can leave tomorrow, if you are ready. We'll get the supplies and horses together today and ride out in the morning at sunrise."

Eric left the meeting with Nantan feeling optimistic about the collaboration. Now, all he had to do was convince Megan of why she'd be better off staying here to wait for him, and though he was sure she would have her objections, he hoped to win Aaron over to his side first and enlist his help. The kid was waiting for him at the general store nearby, and Eric walked over to tell him that his business in town was done and they could head back out to the ranch if he was ready. Aaron had wanted to go to the meeting with him, but Nantan had not invited him, so that had worked out well for Eric.

"I'm sure you can convince him to let us ride with you," Aaron said, when Eric told him that Nantan and a select group of men would be accompanying him on his journey.

"No, I don't think so. This is going to be a reconnaissance mission for them, and there's always the possibility that we will engage with hostiles somewhere along the way. Nantan is choosing men from his security force that have combat experience. This is no place for my daughter, or for you, Aaron."

"But look at what we have been through already, Mr. Branson. We have already had many hostile encounters. I was even taken prisoner and survived, and we have both traveled a great distance through the wilderness."

"I understand that you have, Aaron. I appreciate all that you have done for my daughter, especially convincing her to come here, even if you arrived separately. But as someone who cares about her as I'm sure that you do, you must understand the risks involved in a trip like this. You both made it through those mountains one time, but that is no guarantee you could do it again. We will be traveling light and pushing hard. I have no doubt that Nantan and the men he chooses to go with us are as good as any I've worked with in overseas operations. They've already proven it to me with the ease with which they tracked and captured me."

"I'm good too," Mr. Branson. "I may not be a soldier, but I'm an expert woodsman. I learned from my father and my Uncle Ethan. People think that modern Indians have lost all of the skills of the old ways, but that's simply not true, at least not here. Not all of the knowledge was lost, and many things were passed down that way from father to son, for generations. Even though we can no longer live on the land as hunters and warriors, we take pride in preserving the knowledge. At least a few of us do."

"I believe you, Aaron, and that is why I am counting on you to look out for Megan while I'm away. If I took her with us, then I would be worried about looking out for her all that time too, and it would divide my attention and my focus, which right now is on getting to that cabin to bring Megan's mother, Vicky, and my friend, Jonathan back here. I'm willing to leave Megan in your hands because I know that you are a true friend to her, Aaron, and that you will do everything in your power to protect her. Can you do that for me, sir? Can you accept this as your mission so that I can complete mine swiftly and without worry for her?"

Aaron was silent for a moment as he thought about all that Eric had said. Eric knew he must be disappointed, but he was a smart kid too, and the logic Eric presented to him was unassailable. "Yes sir! You can count on me, Mr. Branson. I'll protect Megan with my life. I was prepared to do that when we left together, and I'll still do it now. I screwed up when I let those guys take me by surprise, and I'm sorry for that, but at least they didn't see Megan. She's a smart girl and brave too. I can't believe she followed them all the way back there in order to know where they were taking me, and then found her way to those soldiers to report it. She is brave, and you must be proud of her."

"Yes, she is, and I'm glad she was able to do what she did. That brings me to my next point. I know those people that took you to their camp were part of the same militia group I encountered farther north, because it was the information I got there that led me to the camp. But tell me; are you certain the men of the attacking force that rescued you were really soldiers? I mean official U.S. military personnel?"

Aaron thought a minute before he answered. "I guess so. I mean they said they were, and they wiped out all those guys in that camp and burned their stuff. They rounded up all of us that were being held there and said they were taking us someplace safe. I have no idea where. I just knew I couldn't go with them though, or I'd never be able to find Megan. I had no idea where she was by then, but I knew I had to go back to where I'd last seen her and go from there. I knew those men wouldn't let me do that, so I took off running into the woods when I had the chance. They even shot at me, but I don't know if they were actually trying to hit me or not. They didn't though, and I felt lucky to get away."

"Did you notice any official looking markings or insignia on their uniforms or their equipment? Flags or anything like that?"

"Man, I honestly don't know, Mr. Branson. I was pretty shaken up, you know. This all happened so fast and it was so unexpected. I didn't really question who they were, because they said they were the good guys and they'd just killed all the bad guys. As far as their uniforms, I don't know. I mean, they were like green camouflage or something, but I didn't pay much attention to them."

"That's okay," Eric said. "I'm just curious."

"Why? Do you think they weren't really soldiers? Maybe another militia group or something?"

"I don't know. After talking to Nantan and your Uncle Ethan, I'm getting a better idea of what's going on out here. I doubt if they were militia, since the strike seemed to correlate with Megan's report of the camp to those soldiers she found at the outpost on the highway, but they may be hired contractors doing work the Army isn't authorized to do, especially considering this is happening on U.S. soil. It's hard to say, and we may never know, but the main reason Nantan wants to go is to learn more of what is going on. It's valuable knowledge that will help him and the rest of the security force here keep your people safe."

"I understand, Mr. Branson. I wish I could go, but I will respect your wishes and stay here with Megan. She may not be too happy about it, but you're right. She'll be safe here."

"Thank you. I'll talk to her when we get back to your uncle's."

Just as he expected, Megan was even more displeased than Aaron when she found out she wasn't going to be included in Eric's expedition to go back to the cabin to get her mom and the others.

"It seems like all I ever do anymore is wait! I'm going to be bored out of my mind sitting here that long!"

"You sound just like your mom! She's had to do a lot of waiting too, but we all have. I know it's not what you'd prefer, but it's best for you and it's best for me this way. We are going to be traveling fast and as hard as we can push the horses, and believe me, it won't be any fun."

"It's still better than sitting here doing absolutely nothing!"

"Well, at least you won't be alone. Aaron is staying with you, so there's that. I like him. He seems like a good guy."

"I like him too, Dad, but now I'm like, what's the point in getting to know him better? You're saying the only option we have is to get on a boat and sail to some faraway island, so I guess I'll never see him again."

"Nothing is certain anymore, Megan. First, I have to go get your mom. I don't know how or when we'll get back to Louisiana, but if Aaron wants to come with us, I don't have a problem with that."

"He won't, because this is his homeland, and these are his people. He's never lived anywhere else besides here on the reservation and in the dorm on campus for that brief time he was there. I doubt he's ever even seen the ocean, much less sailed. So, this will just be another sad good-bye like with every other friend I had."

"Vicky will be coming back here with us. She doesn't have any close family anywhere near here now that her grandparents are dead."

"Yeah, she still has her mom, but she's so far away, I don't know how she would ever get there on her own, but she may want to try."

"If not, she can go with us. The option is there if she wants it."

"How much room do you have on this boat anyway though, Dad? You said Mom wants to go, but if she does, that means Daniel and Andrew will be going too of course, which seems kind of weird, considering that it's your boat. And then there's Grandpa and Uncle Keith. And what about your friend, Jonathan?"

"It may be tight, but there's room to fit everyone that wants to go. I don't think your Uncle Keith will though, because he still feels it's his duty to serve his parish, especially now that they're so shorthanded. And I don't know if your grandpa will go either. I wouldn't be surprised to get back and find him wearing one of those spare badges Keith's department has lying around down there. You know your grandpa. Jonathan's plan was to find a boat and hang around the Atchafalaya where he could fish. I never promised him a ride to the islands, but he's been a hell of a trooper ever since I met him, so I wouldn't tell him no if he's changed his mind. Your stepdad wasn't too happy about any of this, but I think he's had time to make an attitude adjustment. It's none of my business anymore regarding him and your mom, but she's not going to stay there while you and I sail away, you can believe that. So, Daniel is going to have to make his choice."

"Well, the sailing sounds fun and all, but this is way too complicated and not something I'm ready to think about right now. I just hope things settle down first and it doesn't come to that. I'm really more optimistic that they will now, after the way that Army sergeant helped me out by getting me here and then sent troops to attack those guys that took Aaron. I think they're getting it back under control, so that's what I'm counting on."

As long as Megan was willing to stay there on the reservation with Aaron without complaint, Eric saw no reason to burst her bubble, but he didn't share her optimism and saw little reason to alter his long-term plans just yet. He changed the subject and tried to simply enjoy spending what little time he had left with Megan before he had to leave. In the morning he would be up before dawn, checking his weapons and getting Maggie and Sally ready for the journey.

Ten

ERIC MET NANTAN AND the four he'd chosen to accompany them just after sunrise, and the six-man party started out to the north without further ado. In addition to the extra horse Eric was leading, they had three more packhorses with them that could serve as mounts for Shauna, Vicky and Jonathan if for some reason the other horses left at Bob's place were unavailable. Nantan and his men were traveling light; with winter sleeping bags and bivy sacks and as much weight in weapons, magazines and ammunition as their other gear and supplies combined. Eric packed likewise, having already told them of the enormous stockpile of supplies Bob had stored at the cabin. Carrying food for the return journey wasn't really necessary.

They crossed from Jicarilla reservation lands onto adjacent national forest property, and from there the Apaches led the way across a landscape of brush-covered rolling foothills well to the west of the Continental Divide. Nantan said it was a faster route than the high-country trails, and that they knew shortcuts that would avoid most roads altogether.

Still, there were some that had to be crossed, and scattered ranches and communities they had to skirt around, along with barbed wire fences that presented obstacles for the horses. A couple of the men carried wire cutters for the latter, but in the places where it was isolated enough to do so, they used existing cattle gaps to avoid leaving traces of their passage.

"The outsiders moving in are rustling cattle where they can," Nantan told Eric. "Soon, there won't be any left."

"Well, I can see that they would, considering how much ranch country there is out here. I suppose relatively tame cows are a reliable source of meat for those who are too lazy or lack the skills to hunt wild game."

"*Slow elk*," Nantan laughed. "They are easy to kill! And at the rate they're going, most of the herds around here will be wiped out in a couple more months. The range lands out here are too big to patrol, and there are too many desperate people who are hungry. After that, I'm afraid if enough of those outsiders passing through survive long enough, the real elk and other game will become scarce too."

"I've seen it before, in parts of Africa," Eric said. "Never thought I would here though. It still seems so big and wild out here; so lonely in these mountains and deserts."

"Some of it was, when most people still stayed in their cities and towns. But now that they've poured out of the population areas looking for someplace to go, you never know where you're going to find them. Not all of them are bad people of course. Some are just folks with the sense to try and avoid trouble by going where they don't expect to find too many others. The only problem with that though, is that too many of them from all those different places have the same idea."

"And so, they bug out to what they think are safe refuges, only to find them crowded with all the rest who have converged there looking for the same!"

"Exactly."

"That's why we're leaving on a boat; at least if I can get my family back to Louisiana where it's waiting for us."

"You may not be the only one with that idea either. You may find that the paradise you're thinking of is full as well these days."

"Maybe, but putting an ocean crossing between us and the worst of this can't be a bad thing. And I know a few choice islands most people wouldn't associate with paradise. Some that are hard as hell to get to as well."

Nantan was silent for a moment, thinking that over, but then said: "We'll make our stand right here. It may not end well, but I'd rather die here than anywhere else I could think of."

Eric couldn't argue with that concept, but he wasn't attached to a particular piece of land, either here or elsewhere. He'd come so close to dying in so many places that it mattered little to him where it happened when the time finally came. Eric had no fear of death, but none of what he was here for had anything to do with himself. Sure, there were risks for his family regardless of where they went, and no guarantees they'd survive the passage or find refuge on the other side, but weighing the odds, Eric was still inclined to believe it was one of the better options. But he wouldn't make that decision alone, as he had no intention of forcing anyone, including Megan, to do anything they didn't want to do. Eric knew Megan had become attached to Aaron and leaving him behind was going to be hard for her. Vicky was another complication if she decided she wanted to go with them, as Eric hadn't planned on such a big crew. He figured Jonathan would still want to stay in Louisiana, but the kid had been so helpful to him that Eric wasn't looking forward to leaving him behind either. And then there was Shauna and her other family.... Eric stopped himself from thinking that far ahead. Just getting back to Louisiana was going to be challenging enough. Megan had done her best to describe the location of that highway checkpoint where she'd met the helpful sergeant that saw to it that she was taken to the reservation, and Eric intended to start there, once he got Shauna and the others out of the cabin. He would appeal to him and work his way up the chain of command as far as necessary in an attempt to arrange some sort of safe transport for them all. He expected it could be done. After all, Lieutenant Holton had made it happen for getting them out here. Eric didn't talk of any of this with Nantan and his companions though, as they seemed to prefer silence to idle conversation, which suited him perfectly.

Once they had crossed into the state of Colorado, Nantan and his men led Eric on a route that still kept them well to the west of the Continental Divide, but within the big national forests that adjoined one another to create a virtual corridor of wilderness north to south along the backbone of the state. They traveled long hours each day, stopping only when it was too dark to proceed and camping with minimal cooking and other activities that could give their presence away. The gear the Apaches carried was minimal, but all top-quality stuff, including sleeping bags and bivy sacks rated for serious winter camping. These men didn't seem bothered by the cold anyway, and Eric figured they could get by without that stuff if they had to. They were clearly at home living outdoors in conditions that were harsh by any standards.

"It'll be a lot worse in another month," Nantan told Eric. "Good thing you're going now to get them out. That cabin will be cut off in the winter."

Bob Barham had told him as much, and Eric knew it was precisely why the old man had stockpiled so much firewood, as well as food and other supplies. He'd been planning to winter over up there, and there was probably enough for Shauna, Vicky and Jonathan to do the same, but Eric was sure glad they wouldn't have to now. It was already going to be bad enough facing Shauna again, and he fully expected to be on the receiving end of her pent-up fury the moment she laid eyes on him. The good news he had to tell her would soften her up some, of course, but he knew Shauna well enough to know that she wouldn't let him off the hook so easily after what he'd done to her.

Nevertheless, Eric was looking forward to seeing her again, and found himself thinking about her a lot. This was an interesting situation they found themselves in, now that everything had changed here at home and he'd come back to get her and Megan out of danger. Eric had initially hoped to find them all in Florida, of course, and even when he learned he would have to go to Colorado to get Megan, he'd never planned on bringing Shauna here with him. But here she was, and her husband, Daniel, was more than a thousand miles away. Shauna had barely mentioned him since they'd left, and Eric wondered how that would change once she learned that their mission out here was complete, and it was time to go back. Would she look forward to returning to him? Eric didn't know, but he did know that he'd enjoyed the illusion of having his family back, of working together with Shauna as a team, with a common goal of finding their daughter and doing their job as parents to keep her safe.

"It's probably best to use the main trail once we get to here," Eric pointed, as the men crouched around the national forest map Nantan had spread out on the ground before them the next morning. "The approach to the cabin from that direction isn't obvious, but I'm well familiar with it now, and we'll only have to use the trail for a few miles before we turn off again."

"And we'll pass this militia camp where you got the information about where to find Aaron and your daughter?" Nantan asked.

"Yes. It's not far off the trail. They set up there so they could intercept any travelers using that route."

"And you're sure you left none of them alive?" It was Luke who asked. He was the best tracker and woodsman on the security force, according to Nantan. Ethan and Aaron had agreed, when they learned he was going.

"Positive, but you're welcome to have a look around. It isn't far out of our way at all, and you may find something useful."

"We'll see it on the way back from the cabin," Nantan said, looking at Luke. "Let's go there first because we don't want to keep Eric's wife and friends waiting any longer than necessary."

Another day of hard traveling took them to the trail intersection Eric had pointed out on the map. Luke went ahead on point and the rest of them spread out at considerable distance along the path to lessen the chances of the group running into an ambush. It was already late in the afternoon and Eric was unsure if they'd reach the place they would turn off for the descent to the cabin before dark, but then everything changed when they all caught up to Luke. He had dismounted from his horse and was busy studying the ground along the trail and down the slope on the east side.

"What is it?" Nantan asked.

"One horse, and one person, likely a woman, followed the trail to this point from the north, and then turned off and headed down that slope."

Eric and the others dismounted, but Luke waved them back until he was finished studying the sign he found in the snow and in the muddy places in the sunlight where it had melted. Hearing what Luke said, he thought he had a pretty good idea of what it all meant.

"Dammit, Shauna!" He muttered under his breath. *"I should have known you wouldn't be able to wait!"*

"Two days ago," Eric heard Luke say to Nantan.

"Are you sure it was just one woman and a horse?" Eric was trying to make sense of it. Would Shauna leave alone, without Jonathan and Vicky? If so, then why was she walking instead of riding. He knew Jonathan couldn't walk out on his own at this point, and that even if Vicky and Shauna were walking, they would have to take a horse for him, but with so many horses available, why would any of them walk? And why was there only one set of footprints? *None of it added up... unless either Vicky or Shauna was riding on the same horse with Jonathan...*

"Only one woman and one horse," Luke assured him.

"And you're certain it was two days ago? That's long enough that they could be far away by now."

"Yes, give or take a few hours. Here, look at this."

Eric wasn't a tracker, but he understood when Luke pointed out and explained the clues he used to deduce the time frame. "Then we need to get to the cabin as soon as possible and see if Jonathan and Vicky are there," he said. "Shauna may well have taken off on her own. Once we know, do you think it will be possible to track her?"

"Sure, unless she hits a road somewhere and stays on the pavement."

"Maybe you'll find more sign between here and the cabin that will tell you more."

"If it is there, I will find it," Luke assured him.

Eric followed close behind him as Luke backtracked along the trail. Eric didn't have to tell him where the turn-off point was, because Luke found the prints from the woman and horse where they exited the drainage. A short distance down, he found something else.

"They camped here; built a fire. And yes, there was someone else with the woman. A man. Look at this:"

Eric saw the pile of coals and partially burned wood in a narrow slot between two boulders. And the footprints Luke was staring at.

"You said your friend, Jonathan was injured. See here? You can tell where he used a stick or staff of some kind to help him walk."

"Yeah, Bob made him crutches. Are you still sure the other woman wasn't with them?"

"Only one woman and one man so far. You were right, the injured man must be riding the horse while she is walking and leading it. But he dismounted here, of course, because they camped."

"That's another thing that doesn't make any sense at all. Why would they camp so close to the cabin if they were leaving? It's just a short hike down from here, and they could have easily made many more miles after their last night there. We'd better hurry on down there. It'll be dark soon. Hopefully, we'll get the rest of our answers when we get there."

Eric knew something was wrong even before they reached the clearing where the cabin stood, and his companions sensed it too. For one thing, it was too quiet down there, and though they didn't see any smoke wafting up out of the drainage from a fireplace, there was a distinctive smell of a recent burn, but no evidence of a forest fire that he could see. Eric signaled to the others to wait, while he went on ahead. If either Vicky or Shauna were still there, he didn't want to surprise them with the sudden emergence of a band of strangers. But when he reached the area through which he knew he could normally see the cabin through the trees, he could tell that it was gone!

Eric held his weapon at ready and crept closer, using the natural cover as much as possible until he was near enough to see the details. The sight that met his eyes instantly brought to mind that recent day when he and Keith and Bart had likewise discovered Keith's house burned to the ground. Bob Barham's cabin was destroyed, and for a moment, Eric didn't rule out the possibility that it was some accident that perhaps explained the reason they found those foot and hoof prints leading away from here. But then he circled around through the trees for a closer look before stepping out into the open, and that's when he could see that the barn was also burned down, and none of the horses were in sight. He studied the scene from concealment for several minutes, and then turned and waved to Luke and the other Apaches to come ahead. Eric wanted Luke to check the area first, before any sign that he might find there was disturbed, and so they waited while he went ahead of them, taking Wolf, their second most experienced tracker with him.

The two of them checked the rubble first to be sure there were no human or animal remains among what was left of the cabin and barn, and then scoured the ground all around, looking for evidence to complete the story.

"There were many men here, Eric." Luke said, when he waved Eric over, pointing out the obvious boot prints. "Ten at least, maybe more. It's hard to be sure when there's so many, and they were all over the property."

Eric moved closer to the blackened rubble. "How long ago?"

"Two, maybe three days. I'm guessing it was just before the woman and the horse made those tracks out of here."

"So, they escaped whoever did this. But we don't know if they all did. We've got to find out where these men came from, and where they went!" Eric scanned the clearing around the cabin site, and then his eyes fell on something down there in the lower meadow out front and stopped. It was Bob Barham's grave marker that Eric had erected himself, but at the base of it was something that hadn't been there before. He asked Luke to come with him and then headed directly to it. It was a small cairn of rocks about two feet tall, carefully arranged for stability and with purpose, but why? Eric crouched down in front of it, examining the smooth stones that must have been collected from the nearby creek, and that's when he noticed a bit of something plastic under one of them; just the corner of a plastic bag. Eric began moving the stones aside until it was uncovered, and he could see it was definitely a bag, and that the top had been tied in a knot to close it. He could feel something inside and he tore it open to take out a folded piece of a map. At first, he thought there might be a route or something marked on the map, but seeing nothing there, he turned it over and found Vicky's note on the back.

Eric read the message through twice, taking in what it said as he knelt there beside the grave marker. Men that may have been soldiers had come here, and they had taken Shauna and all but one of the horses away. They had also taken all of the guns and supplies and then set the fires that burned the cabin and barn. Vicky and Jonathan had escaped because they hadn't been there when the men arrived, and they had Tucker because they had taken him with them that morning because of Jonathan's broken leg. The part of the note that Eric kept reading over again was the last part that said the two of them had followed after the men only to find the other horses shot dead and a trail that ended where vehicle tracks began. Vicky had sketched a rough map to the place, down the creek and then right on a gravel road to another turn off. She said they had returned here and found a small survival cache Bob had left nearby, and with that and Tucker, the two of them had left to make their way to the Jicarilla reservation, in hopes of finding Eric there.

"Dammit!" Eric cursed as he got to his feet, the note in his hand. Lucas and Nantan and the others were all gathered around him by now, anxious to hear what the message said. "The footprints you saw were Vicky's. She was leading an Appaloosa gelding called Tucker, and my friend Jonathan was riding him because he still can't walk. And my ex-wife has been taken away by the men that were here. Vicky and Jonathan saw it happen and saw them take everything from the cabin before they burned it. She counted thirteen of them, but there may be more. They followed them, hoping to find a way to rescue Shauna, but they had trucks hidden near a road down in the valley and from there, they drove away. I can find the place where they had them parked." Eric held up the sketch Vicky drew at the bottom of her note. "When Vicky and Jonathan saw that they couldn't help Shauna, they decided to try and make it to the reservation to tell me. All of you should go on back there as well. Maybe you can catch up with them along the way. I appreciate your help getting here, but I'll continue alone from here and see what I can find."

"No way are we letting you do that alone, brother. Without Luke, I doubt you'd be able to find them, and even if you did, you'd be far outnumbered. Wolf will track the girl and the young man and escort them safely back to the reservation once he catches up to them. Their trail should be easy to follow, and they are moving slow. Besides, he knows where they are headed. The rest of us will go with you. Luke will be our tracker, and all of us will have your back when we find those bastards who took your wife."

"We don't know that they aren't soldiers," Eric said. "But if they are, they are a disgrace to the uniform. Vicky said they shot all the horses once they got the guns and other goods loaded into their trucks."

"Then let's go to that place at first light in the morning and see if we can determine what they did after that. We'll camp here now, and Wolf will go in the morning too when we leave."

Eleven

IT WAS A LONG night for Eric, as he was impatient to get going to find Shauna's last known location that Vicky had described. He would have preferred to go ahead and travel there in the dark, despite the cold, but Luke had persuaded him otherwise, saying they might miss something along the trail that could prove to be valuable information. Luke wanted to arrive there in daylight, with time to scour the area for clues before the rest of them converged on it. Eric was grateful for Vicky's note and all the information it contained, but it was really bad news to learn that the men had switched to vehicles such a short distance away. Vicky and Jonathan couldn't follow beyond that point, and Eric doubted Luke could either. But the Apache tracker said it wasn't necessarily a lost cause.

"The good thing is that it's only been three days. There may not be much sign at all, but what there is will mostly still be there."

Those three short days were enough to change everything though, and it made Eric sick to think he'd been so close to getting here on time. He'd traveled fast and arrived at the reservation as soon as humanly possible, given the conditions and the business he had to take care of along the way, but then he'd made a big mistake with the way he entered Jicarilla land. His arrest and interrogation had cost him as many days as that, while Megan was already there all along. If not for that unnecessary delay, he might have made it back here sooner, but in hindsight, he realized now he should have simply brought Shauna, Vicky and Jonathan with him. He'd expected to face her fury over that when he arrived here, but now he was facing something far worse: the reality that she was missing and maybe even dead because of what he'd done. Eric didn't want to think about what might have happened to her since she'd been taken, and the truth was that he might never know. He was grateful for the help he was getting from Luke, but still skeptical they would find much beyond what Vicky had already discovered.

He had a final word with Wolf at dawn before the man left, giving him a message for Jonathan and Vicky, and wishing him luck. Wolf was confident he'd be able to find them and that he'd catch up to them long before they reached the reservation, especially since Vicky was on foot. Wolf took one of the extra horses they'd brought with them so that the three of them could all ride when he found them, and he told Eric and the others that they would be waiting at the reservation until they returned. As he rode away, Luke was already making his way down the creek on the trail of the raiders, and Eric and Nantan followed behind, along with the remaining two men of their party, Tommy and Red.

They worked their way through the forested creek basin on foot, leading their horses and stopping occasionally when Luke found something of interest that he wanted to investigate closer. When they reached the road where Vicky said the men had turned north, Luke and Eric went on ahead while the others brought up the rear from a sufficient distance to react in case they encountered anyone on the road. All was quiet that morning though, at least until they came to the dead-end turn off that Vicky had mapped out in her sketch and heard the noise of a large flock of crows.

"They've come for the feast," Luke said, as they rode down the narrow two track and saw dozens of the black birds flying into the nearby trees, annoyed at the human interruption. Other scavengers had gotten to the dead horses as well, Eric saw, and Luke pointed out large coyote tracks when they dismounted. The tracker's real interest though, was in the tire tread marks he found around the turnabout and leading to and from the road.

"Can you tell how many vehicles they had?" Eric asked.

"At least three, maybe four. All light trucks or maybe SUVs. Mud-grip or semi-off-road tires. I can't tell the brand without something to compare them to, but I can remember what they look like if we find more tread marks like this where we're going next."

"And where is that?" Eric asked. "How are we supposed to know where in the hell to go next now that we know they left here using roads? There may be some tracks on the gravel, but eventually this road will come out on pavement. And then there'll be nothing."

"True, but at least we know they came in on the gravel and went back out the same way. We'll study the maps we have, and see where it crosses the next road, and then go there and have a look around."

Eric couldn't argue with that as a logical step, but it still wasn't much to go on. After determining from the map that the gravel road came to a T-intersection with a bigger road several miles to the north, they plotted a cross-country route that would take them there directly and with little chance of being seen. When they reached a ridge overlooking this junction, they saw that the other road was indeed paved, and Eric's doubts were reinforced. But Luke told them to give him a few minutes while he went down alone on foot to see if he could find any clues to tell him which way the trucks had turned. It had to be either east or west, as there were no other options.

"Definitely west," he said when he rejoined them. One of the trucks cut the corner just enough to make clear marks in the gravel that it came that way either going out or coming in.

I didn't find any sign like that indicating any of them cut to the eastbound side. But they are on pavement now, so this is where the tire tracks end."

"And there's nothing we can do, other than maybe follow the paved road west and hope we get lucky? They could be clear across the state by now, or beyond."

"Yes, they could. But there's also the possibility that we'll find another road they turned off on. Or that they'll come back this way and we'll see them when they do."

Eric knew either was a long shot, but what else was he to do? He had to make every effort he could to find Shauna, or else he'd never convince Megan to leave the country with him. Of course, he didn't want to leave Megan's mom behind anyway, for any reason. The only way he would even consider doing that was if he knew for a fact she was dead, and he knew he probably wouldn't know until he found the men who'd taken her away.

"We can follow the edge of this plateau for a few miles," Nantan said, pointing to the map he'd unfolded again while they talked. "From up there we should be able to see any traffic that passes through the valley on that road."

"At least until it starts climbing again at this pass," Eric was looking at a series of switchbacks indicating the route farther west.

"For that part, we'd best wait for dark."

By midafternoon, they'd gone as far as they could without having to use the road again. They dismounted on the south slope close to where it began climbing out of the valley, and then took a break and rested the horses as they waited for darkness. It was an hour later, while they were quietly eating, before getting ready to move out again, that they heard the sound of approaching vehicles coming through the valley from the east.

Eric watched through his binoculars as a grey crew cab pickup and two identical black SUVs traveling close together approached and finally passed their position. They were all civilian vehicles, the SUVs looking nearly new, with their shiny factory paint and windows tinted so darkly that Eric couldn't see the drivers or other occupants inside them. Their passage along the road here could be related to the men that took Shauna, or it could mean nothing at all. It was impossible to tell at this point. For several minutes after they disappeared from sight, they could hear the sound of their motors as the vehicles worked their way back and forth up the switchbacks to the top of the pass. When the sounds died away, it was time for them to follow, as it was the way they were going anyway, and Eric could only hope that if anyone else came along while they were up there that there would be a place to leave the road with the horses before they were caught in the headlights.

The temperature plummeted rapidly after dark and the wind at the top of the pass made the cold dangerous, but the Apaches didn't seem bothered by it and Eric wasn't about to acknowledge that he was in front of them. Night was the only feasible option for following this road, as the terrain presented no other routes through the pass that the horses could negotiate. They pressed on once they reached the summit and began a long winding descent down the west side through miles of heavy forest that finally gave way to a more open, brushy country with scattered pines and cedars growing at the lower elevations. It was here that they came to another gravel road that turned off the pavement to the north, and Luke dismounted to use his flashlight to study the first fifty feet or so of gravel.

"There's been a lot of traffic in and out of here," he said. "Come and see this."

Eric walked over to see what he was shining his light on in an area of wet silty ground where the gravel was thin, and saw distinct, well-defined tire tread marks.

"This is the same pattern we saw at the place where they killed the horses. It doesn't mean it was them, but it's the same brand and model tire. Where does this road go? Does the map show it?"

"Yes," Nantan said, as he joined them, squatting down to lay it out under Luke's light so he could see it. "It may be outdated, but it shows that this first turn off west of the pass runs north eight miles to a dead end. It shows a forest service work station up there."

"Which would definitely be closed now, if it wasn't already," Eric said.

"Yes, of course, but that doesn't mean someone's not using it."

"Someone is definitely using this road," Luke said, "and recently too. Look at this; these tracks are fresh. Made tonight."

"Maybe the truck and the two SUVs we just saw earlier?"

"Maybe. We haven't seen any other traffic, so it seems likely to me."

"Then we should follow this road a short distance and find a place to wait for daylight. Then, we can watch for any traffic coming in or out in the morning and maybe one or two of us can recon that work center and see if anything is going on there."

They found a place where the gravel road crossed a low ridge just a couple miles north of the pavement and then set up on a brushy hill that would afford a view of the road from both directions after sunup. Eric was wired, as he was excited about this new development, so he agreed to take the first watch while the other men got a couple hours of sleep. He would get a brief nap before dawn if possible, but even if he didn't, Eric was ready and anxious for what the coming day might bring. If those tire tracks really were one and the same as the ones they'd found where he knew the men left with Shauna in their vehicles, then there was hope that he might learn where they took her. Eric was going to make somebody talk if he suspected they had answers. And if he couldn't think of a way to do it, he was sure the four Apache warriors with him would help him think of something.

Building a fire was out of the question of course, so the only respite from the cold that Eric got was the short hour and a half he spent in his sleeping bag after Red, the quietest and most reserved of the four Apaches, relieved him of his watch. When he crawled back out at dawn, he guessed the temperature was somewhere in the low teens, if not the single digits. His companions still seemed unfazed though, and Eric knew it came from a lifetime of living in the mountains and working outdoors on the range before they joined the military to spend yet more time in harsh conditions as special forces operators. It was good to be in the company of men such as these again, and Eric was beginning to feel like he was part of a team once more, despite getting off on the wrong foot with them in his initial introduction.

Once the sun was up, its warmth brought rapid relief from the chill, and the five of them picked spots on the hillside where they could take advantage of it while still remaining concealed from anyone passing by on the road below. Two hours passed with nothing breaking the silence but the screech of a hawk circling high overhead, and then everything changed when Luke alerted them with a low whistle and Eric looked at where he was pointing to see a plume of dust around the next bend in the road to the north. The more open country here afforded a good view for nearly a mile, and Eric waited as he trained his binoculars on the moving dust until the source of it rounded the bend. The first vehicle was a pickup truck, followed by two SUVs that he thought could well be the same two they'd seen the afternoon before on the other side of the pass. A fourth vehicle was following the SUVs now though, and he saw that like the one in front, it was a four-door pickup truck.

They were moving fairly slow on the rough gravel road, and it was several minutes before they passed by, the occupants unaware that they were being watched. Eric could clearly see the driver and two other men through the windows of the lead pickup. They were wearing camouflage BDUs of some kind, but the truck was an ordinary Ford F250, gray in color with no markings of any kind. He'd caught a glimpse of a driver and front seat passenger through the windshield of one of the SUVs too, but the dark windows blocked any view of the rear seats or cargo areas. The only other thing that stood out about the two SUVs was the absence of license plates on the rear of either one, while the Ford had a plate that was so covered in dust it was impossible to tell which state had issued it. Bringing up the rear was a silver Dodge Ram, and Eric saw two men in the front seat of it as well. That truck was cleaner, and when it went by, he could clearly see it bore Texas plates.

There were places where the road to the south was out of view behind the hills, but the dust the trucks kicked up made it easy to keep track of their progress until they crossed another open area where they were in plain view again, still maintaining their slow, but steady speed. Luke looked back at Eric and the others and signaled that he was going down there to check the sign in the road. As he went on ahead, the rest of them moved closer as well, eager to learn if Luke found a match. It took him a few minutes to find a clean tire track from the pickup that the two SUVs following hadn't driven over, but when he did, Luke gave a thumbs up.

"This tread from the gray Ford is the same as one of those from the place they killed the horses. It may be a coincidence, but that seems unlikely to me now, especially after seeing those guys dressed like soldiers, the way the girl described them."

Eric glanced back to where he'd last seen the truck, leading the SUVs south. All were out of sight now, obviously headed to the paved road, where they would leave no trail that could be followed. The only thing left to do was to continue their plan to recon that work station and see what was going on there. He was almost certain they would find more evidence there, and likely more of those men, who were possibly using it as a base of operations. The five of them gathered around the map again to study the terrain in order to decide the best approach, as they obviously didn't want to use the road. They had decided on a couple of possibilities when Tommy, who had walked back up the hill a bit, called out to get their attention.

"One of those trucks is coming back! I think it's the Dodge!"

"Just one of them?"

"Yes. That's all I see. The rest must have turned onto the road."

Eric knew it was time to make a decision. This was an unexpected opportunity they needed to take advantage of, but in order to do so, they had to act fast. "Keep an eye on it and make sure the others don't come back too!" he called back to Tommy, before turning to Nantan, Luke and Red: "We need to stop that truck and get some answers. We know the work center is still a few miles to the north, far enough that no one there will know if we act fast."

"As long as more of them don't come out the same way," Nantan said.

"That could happen but cutting these two off in an isolated area like this seems easier than questioning someone at a possible outpost of unknown strength. We need to find out who these people are, and if they were involved in the raid on the cabin."

"I agree," Nantan said. "Do you want to block the road? Shoot out their tires when they go by, or what?"

"No, I want to flag them down; alone. I'll be walking down the road when they get here, apparently unarmed and looking lost and desperate. You and your men will be covering me from up there and across the road too. They'll probably stop and try to detain me. Then, you'll have them."

"Unless they open fire on you without asking questions first."

"That's possible, but I trust that you'll have my back. I'd rather not have any gunplay at all. It'll be much better if we can do this quickly and quietly, but one way or the other, I think we should take the chance."

Nantan agreed and after quickly scanning the available nearby cover, called to Tommy to remain on the higher ground and be ready with his rifle. Luke would take a low position on the opposite side of the road, while Nantan and Red crouched behind the nearest concealing bushes they could find next to where Eric would step into the roadway. The horses were still well-hidden from view in the trees higher up the hillside, and Eric stashed his rifle behind a nearby boulder, keeping only his Glock on him, concealed in his belt under his jacket. Using dirt from the side of the road, he did his best to look the part of a lost and desperate man, smearing it on his face and clothing and into his disheveled hair.

He could hear the truck coming by the time he was ready, the automatic transmission shifting gears as it pulled up the steep grade just to the south. Eric didn't look back at Nantan or the others. His attention was focused on the sound, and he walked down the middle of the road with a sudden urgency, as a man looking for a second chance at survival might be inclined to do upon hearing the arrival of potential help. When the truck finally rolled into view just fifty yards away, Eric stopped right where he was in the middle of the road and began waving his arms to flag it down, making it obvious he was desperate for help.

The driver hit the brakes at the unexpected sight and skidded on the gravel, causing the truck to fishtail a little and almost go off the steep shoulder before it came to a stop. Then the passenger side door flew open and the other man stepped out with his handgun drawn, pointing it at Eric as he took up position behind the door.

"FREEZE RIGHT WHERE YOU ARE! KEEP THOSE HANDS UP WHERE I CAN SEE THEM!"

"I just need help!" Eric said. "I need water! Do you have any water?"

Now the driver exited the vehicle as well, slamming the door shut behind him. He had drawn his pistol too, and he and his partner advanced in Eric's direction.

"How did you get here? Where did you come from?"

"I don't know! I'm lost! I didn't know this road was here until I stumbled onto it from down there." Eric nodded in the direction of the brush-covered valley to the east. "I just need water. And a ride to the nearest town, if you can take me, so I can get home!"

"This is a private road, and you're trespassing on private property! We're going to give you a ride all right, but first, you need to get face down on the road, and then put your hands behind your back!"

Eric didn't argue with him and complied immediately. He wanted both of these men to keep their full attention focused on him, trusting that his new-found warrior brothers would take care of the rest before the one walking over to him managed to get the zip tie he'd pulled from his pocket into place around his wrists.

Twelve

ERIC FELT THE SHARP pressure and the weight of a knee in his back as the man who'd approached him circled around behind him to secure his hands while the other covered him from near the front of the truck. He pretended to be confused as to why they were detaining him, still asking for water and a ride to keep their attention centered on him and away from their surroundings. As the one on top of him worked to pull his wrists together, Eric saw movement out of the corner of his eye, and then the weight was suddenly gone as Nantan's body slammed into the man from one side, carrying him hard into the loose gravel of the road. Eric sprang to his feet in time to see that Red had taken care of the driver, who was now disarmed and in a choke hold from behind. He glanced back to see Nantan on top of the other man, his knife already at the man's throat. The situation seemed to be under control and Eric was about to collect both of the pistols when gunshots rang out from the direction of the pickup. He saw Red and the man he was restraining both go down as bullets punched through the windshield.

Eric dove for the ground as he reached for his Glock. There was someone else in the truck, probably in the back seat, firing at them through the glass! But before Eric could get into position to return fire, multiple rifle shots erupted from the hillside and incoming bullets tore through sheet metal and glass, putting an end to the gunfire from the truck. The shooter inside was neutralized, so Eric turned his attention back to Red and the other man just as he saw that Nantan had subdued his adversary with a heavy blow of his fist.

The shooter inside the truck had been using a pistol, Eric knew that from the sound of the reports. He had gotten off several rounds before Tommy and Luke took him out, and Eric now saw that Red was hit; sitting on the ground and holding pressure on his upper arm, where a dark stain was spreading in the fabric of his coat sleeve beneath his fingers. The man he'd been restraining was less fortunate. He'd taken friendly fire from his buddy in the truck who tried to rescue him, and the round that went through the back of his head was lights out for him.

Tommy and Luke had ceased firing by the time Eric made this assessment, but they were still covering the truck with their rifles. Eric crawled to the front passenger's side fender and waited until Luke gave him the thumbs up signal

159

from his side of the road, as he could apparently see from his position that the shooter was no longer a threat. Eric verified this with a quick check of the back seat, finding a dead man there dressed in the same BDUs as his two companions, and a 9mm Beretta on the floorboard under him, where it had fallen. Eric grabbed the weapon, furious at himself for making such a dumb mistake. This third guy they didn't anticipate could have killed Red as well as Nantan and himself. He hadn't seen anyone in the back seat when the truck passed before, but Eric figured the man must have been there all along, maybe napping or ducking down out of sight as soon as the driver and the other guy up front saw Eric standing in the road. He missed getting a fatal hit on Red, probably because he was too hasty when he began firing, and he'd killed one of his on instead because Red had unwittingly pulled the man into the line of fire when he got hit. Now they had two dead men of unknown association on their hands, and only one left alive that might be able to give them the answers they sought. They needed to get the bodies and the truck off the road, but when Eric walked around to the driver's side, he saw that Tommy had shot holes in both the front and rear tires.

"What'd you do that for?" Eric asked him, when he and Luke made their way down to the road.

"Just making sure no one got away, you know. I wasn't sure how many were in the truck. I just shot the shit out of it as soon as that guy started firing."

Eric figured it didn't really matter. There was no place in the immediate vicinity to get it off the road and hide it anyway. They would just have to hope another vehicle didn't come along before they were done here. Tommy helped him put the two bodies in the bed of the truck though, at least getting them out of sight, while Luke went to assist Red with his wound. There were three mil-spec select-fire M4s in the vehicle in addition to the handguns the men had been carrying, and Eric put them across the hood and then went through the glove box to see what he could find. The truck was registered to a consulting firm in Texas he'd never heard of, and there was nothing to indicate any government or military affiliation. He'd seen enough by now to know though, that these men were professionals, and not some loosely organized civilian militia group. Further digging through the center console revealed that he was right, and Eric cursed under his breath as he stared at the I.D. badges he found in there among the papers and cigarette packs. He'd suspected the men were contractors, but he had not expected to find *this* outfit working here in the U.S. C.R.I. was one of the more notorious private contractor companies he'd ever run across, and their operators had been involved in atrocities in certain countries that made even ISIS terrorists look like the good guys. Eric had been contacted by them on more than one occasion, and though their offers exceeded anything he'd ever earned in his life, he hadn't entertained the idea of accepting one even for a minute. What they were doing here he had no idea, but he knew that if they had men working here, it had to be at least as lucrative as the abundant work available to them in Europe and elsewhere.

"You got any idea who they are?" Tommy asked, as he came back over to see what Eric had found, admiring the nice rifles. "Are they working for the cartels?"

"If I had to guess, I'd say so, yes, because it would take that kind of money to hire them. C.R.I. is a contracting company that's known for dirty work; willing to do most anything if the price is right."

"Too bad we had to kill those two before you could question them."

"Don't worry about it. We got one of them alive. That's all we need if we can make him talk."

"Oh, we can make him talk, brother. Leave that part to us if you like."

Eric followed Tommy over to where Luke and Nantan were talking to Red, his arm now bandaged, and the bleeding stopped.

"It didn't hit any bones," Luke said. "And it went all the way through."

"Yeah, just a flesh wound, man," Red agreed. "I won't say it doesn't hurt like hell, but I'm lucky, I guess. A lot luckier than the dude I was choking out."

"What about him? Has he said anything yet?" Eric looked at Nantan and nodded at the prisoner. He was standing with his back against a small tree, his hands restrained behind it with one of his own zip ties he'd intended to use on Eric.

"Nothing other than calling us a bunch of murderers and bandits for killing his buddies."

"They are C.R.I. contractors if the I.D. badges I found in the truck are legit."

Like Tommy, Nantan had never heard of the company. None of these men had worked in the business after leaving the active military, so they were unaware of what went on in that world.

"I'll fill you in later, and we'll find out who's paying them to be here, but I think Luke's right about the tire tread match. Knowing their standard operating procedure, burning the cabin and taking civilian hostages is about what I would expect. Now, we just have to find out what they did with Shauna."

The prisoner refused to give his name, tell them who he was with, or acknowledge that he'd ever seen Shauna or knew anything of her. He was being a real tough guy, despite

Nantan's warning that holding out on them was going to cause him severe pain.

"We want to know if you're using the forest service work center at the end of this road for your base of operations," Eric said. "We're quite certain that you are, and I want you to tell me how many civilian captives you're holding there and how many men are manning that post."

"The only thing I'm telling you is that you can go straight to hell!"

Eric turned to Nantan. "I'll leave this to you. We don't have time to waste though. They're probably expecting that truck back any minute."

Nantan turned to the prisoner. "My people were at war with almost everyone who wasn't Apache for hundreds of years; other Indian tribes, the Mexicans, and the white settlers and their soldiers. In that time, they learned interesting ways to punish their enemies and make them suffer and die slowly. Sometimes, they would hang you upside down and build a small fire under your head and roast you alive… or strip you naked while the women used their knives to peel the skin from your body, inch-by-inch while you are still alive… But we don't have time for games such as those right now, and there are faster ways to die that are almost as painful too. "Tommy! Bring your horse and your rope!"

Eric was standing off to one side, letting Nantan handle this, but he could see in the hapless man's eyes that he was

164

getting nervous. There was something serious in the hard lines of Nantan's rugged face that offered no illusions that he was joking or that he would be merciful. When Tommy returned, leading his horse and carrying a lasso in his other hand, he passed the noose to Nantan while Luke sliced away the strap that held the man to the tree. Before he could react, Nantan threw him to the ground and had a loop of rope around his ankles that Tommy quickly pulled tight, before climbing into the saddle and wrapping the other end around the horn. At Nantan's nod, he urged his mount forward until the rope went taut when the horse was about fifteen feet away.

"Why don't we take a shortcut to that work center, Tommy? Maybe across those rocks over there:" Nantan began walking that way, and Tommy kept pace with the horse, dragging the man behind him by his feet. He was going slow, and for the first few yards, they were still on the gravel road that was fairly smooth. But the area Nantan pointed to was covered in broken rocks of all sizes and shapes, many of them with sharp edges or abrasive, rough surfaces. When Tommy reached this area on his horse, he maintained the steady walking pace, ignoring the curses of the man he was pulling behind him. Seeing that this technique was likely to be quite effective, Eric followed close behind them, watching as the man's body bounced over the irregular surface and his jacket and shirt rode up from the waist, exposing his flesh to whatever it came into contact with.

"We can go for miles like this," Nantan said, as he walked alongside the unfortunate captive. But pretty soon, there will be little bits of you all over the ground behind us. You'll bleed to death eventually, but it will take a long time, maybe even longer than it will take for the coyotes to follow the blood after we cut you loose."

Eric smiled. His Apache friend's method was brutal and savage but proved quite effective. They'd only gone a few more yards before the man began begging Nantan to stop, saying that he would tell them everything he knew. Nantan told Tommy to stop his horse, but he made no move to untie the man's feet or let him up.

"What is your name and who do you work for?"

"Wilson! My name's Dwight Wilson. I work for C.R.I. It's a security contracting company."

Eric stepped in at this point, squatting down next to the man and grabbing him by the collar. "Okay, Wilson! You and your crew burned a cabin and barn about 20 miles southeast of here. And you took the woman that was there. Why did you do it, and where is she?"

"I don't know man! I wasn't there when they did that. I've been on guard detail at our camp."

Eric looked up at Nantan and Tommy. "Maybe we didn't drag him far enough yet... or maybe not fast enough?"

Tommy nudged his horse forward until the rope went taunt again and the man began sliding slowly across the rocks. When he sped up to a trot, it was only seconds before Wilson was screaming for him to stop.

"Okay! Okay! I wasn't with them on the patrol, but I do know about the woman! They brought her back with them along with a big stash of weapons and supplies. Chief locked her up in the supply room, but she's gone now."

"Gone where, Wilson?" Eric grabbed him again, jerking him up to a sitting position. "Where did they take her?"

"I don't know! I saw them put her in one of the vehicles that just left. I don't know why."

"You mean one of those two black SUVs that you and your buddies were following out of here earlier?"

"Yes. It's our standard protocol. Our job was to follow the convoy out to the pavement and return to base, mainly to report back that the road in here is clear. Our guys in the other pickup truck are escorting them to their destination, I think to another post of ours about a hundred miles south of here, in New Mexico."

Eric couldn't believe what he was hearing. If the woman the man had seen get into one of those vehicles was Shauna, then she'd had passed within mere yards of him less than a half hour prior. If only he'd known, he and Nantan's men could have stopped the entire convoy. Now, they had a huge head start and the one vehicle they *had* stopped was disabled, with two flat tires.

"Who are the people in the black SUVs? Why do they need an escort?"

"Because they're here, man! Nobody moves on the roads in this area without our permission. We're working to lock down this entire sector and move all civilians out. That's what we're here for. We're doing the work the military can't do— like always!"

Eric wasn't sure he believed this. The Army had established checkpoints on many of the highways to the east and north of here, he already knew that. Their operations might be limited in the remote mountain areas for now, but if they were hiring private contracting companies to help reestablish law and order, it would seem that the more populated areas would be a higher priority.

"Okay, but I'm asking you again. Who were the people in the black SUVs and why did they take the woman with them?"

"I would tell you if I knew man, but that's way over my pay grade. All I know is that they were speaking Spanish to each other. They may have been Mexicans, I don't know. Chief was the one dealing with them. I just keep my mouth shut and follow orders, like everyone else here."

"Yeah, I'll bet you do! So, it's like I've heard. You and your fellow C.R.I. mercs are the hired guns on this side of the border for the drug cartels that are moving north, right? And those guys were some of your clients! So why did they take the woman with them?"

"I really don't know! Chief would have to tell you that. We don't keep prisoners though, because we're not set up for that. Most of the civilians we've relocated have been sent to the government refugee centers! Maybe that's where they were taking her too. But I really don't know man!"

"We're not set up for keeping prisoners either," Eric said, leaning close to glare into the man's eyes. "You're going to tell me everything I want to know about this outpost of yours at the end of the road, and this 'chief' who is in charge of it. Either that, or we finish this now and leave you in the back of that truck with your two partners. First, I want to know how many men are present there, and what the security detail consists of and what weapons they have at that post."

"I *am* part of the security detail! Me and the two guys that were with me. There's a gate near the end of the road, with a guard watching it while we were away. We were supposed to go right back there after we turned around. Normally two guys are assigned to watch the entrance and the other two patrol the perimeter every couple of hours. But it's been quiet here, so Chief has cut us some slack. It's not like anyone ever comes down this road, at least not until today. They're going to wonder now though. We should have been back by now."

"Why don't you have comms? A radio in your truck? Or a handheld?" Eric had noticed a tall whip antenna mounted on the top of the cab of the other pickup, but there wasn't a two-way in the one Tommy had shot up, and Eric had found no handheld units on the dead men or Wilson either. "I saw an antenna on the other truck."

"Yes, there's a radio in most of our trucks, but not the Dodge. It wasn't part of our regular fleet. We didn't need comms anyway, because we were only going out to the road and back, like I told you."

"Is there a base station and tower at the compound?" Eric was thinking fast. If there was a commercial-band radio system in place, gaining control of it might be Shauna's best hope.

"Yes. It was already there from when the forest service used the place. Our technician converted it to our secure frequency. We've established contact with all our posts out here via repeaters that we've brought back online."

"So, it's possible to reach the crew of the other truck from that base station even out of normal range." Eric smiled. "What about direct contact with the nearest military post?"

"The truck maybe, but the nearest Army post is on the other side of the Continental Divide. We have other stations of our own that are closer when we have something to report to them, but from here, no."

"Because they're not really who you're working for anyway are they? All of that is just a facade to give your outfit a reason to be here, and a reason to be left alone to do whatever in the hell you want."

"I'm just paid to do my job, man. Like everybody else."

"Like your two coworkers down there in the back of that truck with holes in them," Eric said. "I wonder what they'd tell you, if you could ask them if the pay was worth it? I'm not going to shoot you right now, Wilson, but if the information you've given me isn't the truth, I will when I come back."

"We don't need him," Nantan said.

"Not really, but he *did* talk, so there's that. And you know, I may have a little job for him before we hit that compound." Eric was lost in thought for a moment.

"Is that what you have in mind?" Nantan asked. "Taking the compound?"

"I don't see any better options. That truck is disabled, and we can't catch that convoy on horses. I'm thinking of asking this 'chief' fellow to give his guys in that escort truck a call. He can tell them there's been a change of plans and that they need to bring the convoy to a stop and return to base with the woman. Have you got a better idea?"

"I can't think of one," Nantan admitted.

"You know, you and your men have done more than enough, once again. I can't expect you to engage with these assholes and put yourselves at risk for something that is my fight."

"It's our fight too, brother. I told you that already. Now we know for sure that we are dealing with people who are supporting the takeover of these lands. That's one of the reasons why we came with you, to find out who and where they are. It will be an honor to help you kill more of them, if that is what it takes to get back your wife."

Thirteen

NANTAN'S ANSWER WAS THE one Eric had been hoping for, even though he wouldn't have asked him to if he and his men didn't volunteer to help. The biggest thing working against him now was time, because the farther away they took Shauna, the lesser his chances of stopping them. Eric knew he had to move, and now. There was no time for real reconnaissance or to formulate a detailed plan. He had to rely on the information his one source had given him, and now that they were going forward with this immediately, Eric decided to make the man a part of the plan, or at least the main diversion that would give them the edge they needed to get in there and secure that radio.

The necessity of taking out some of the men posted at the work station turned compound was a given. Eric had no qualms about launching a proactive attack on them, knowing what he knew now about their activities here, not to mention what he already knew of this outfit's reputation. But aside from that, they'd taken Shauna against her will, burned Bob Barham's cabin, stolen all their weapons and supplies and killed helpless horses in cold blood. If any group he'd encountered since coming back here deserved the full fury of Eric's wrath, it was these C.R.I. contractors upon which he was about to unleash it. A quick pow-wow with Nantan and his men was enough to proceed with it, despite the lack of recon. Nantan fully understood his part:

"We'll use our horses to close the gap and then get them off the road before we're in sight of the entrance. I'll take Tommy with me and circle around to the north, and Luke and Red can close from the south. You'll have the full attention of the guys manning the gate, and while they're trying to figure out what in the hell is going on, I'll pick them off as I can with this."

Eric eyed the black rifle Nantan had taken from the case strapped onto his packhorse. It was a suppressed Ruger 10/22 rimfire carbine, fitted with an oversized variable power scope. Eric knew it was a precision weapon, capable of pinpoint accuracy with a very low sound signature, but it required getting in really close to be effective, and he commented on this, even though he knew it wasn't news to Nantan.

"Don't worry about that part," Nantan said. "Remember what happened when you tried to sneak across our land? I can get close without being seen."

Eric did, and he knew this little band of modern-day warriors that made up the Jicarilla security force prided themselves on working to recreate the stealthy fighting skills the word 'Apache' had become synonymous with. And to a man, they all had a background in special forces that also gave them the contemporary training and experience that made them even more deadly.

"The little .22 doesn't pack much punch, but if I put it into the side of a man's head or neck from inside of 40 or 50 yards, it'll do the job."

Eric knew it would, because he'd used similar weapons himself for special applications. If Nantan could quickly reduce the number of adversaries they were facing and stop the guards from raising the alarm, it would be quick work to mop up the rest with the M4s when the shit hit the fan. The key to the whole thing though was showing up at that entrance with something totally unexpected, and that was where this Wilson fellow came in. Eric warned him before they moved out that his participation was the only thing keeping him alive, and he promised the man that if he did as he was told and didn't try to help his friends resist what was coming, then he would let him live when they left there to do what they had to do next. Complying with all of this was the only way he would be afforded that luxury though, and Eric could see the understanding in the man's eyes when he reiterated that truth.

They forced him to climb up into the saddle of one of the horses and then Eric mounted his own, taking the reins of the other to lead it as he set out down the road with the Apaches. The extra time that had passed since the convoy left was a bit of a concern, but Wilson said the guards at the gate wouldn't be too worried if the second truck wasn't back immediately. The three of them that had left in it were off duty after that detail, and he said the men sometimes enjoyed a break from the compound when they had a chance and that the guards would probably assume they'd stopped for a smoke and bullshit session. Even so, Eric didn't want to waste any more time than necessary getting there. The group set out at a fast pace, knowing that if anyone from the compound came looking for the missing three, they would be in a motor vehicle that could be heard in time to react. But they had no encounter on the road, and when they had reached the point on the map where they'd decided that Nantan and his men would leave their horses and go on foot, Eric waited with Wilson, giving the Apaches the agreed on five minutes to reach their positions on either side of the compound.

Eric had secured Wilson's wrists in front of him with one of the many zip ties he found in the cargo pockets of his BDUs, and several turns of cord through that secured the plastic tie to the saddle horn. When they started moving again, Eric's rifle was behind him, out of sight, while his Glock was in its holster under his coat, easy to access but hidden from view as he and Wilson rode two abreast down the middle of the road.

When they rounded the bend and came into view of the chain-link perimeter fence and gate, Eric urged his horse forward, unperturbed by the sight of the two armed guards that stood up from where they'd been sitting and reached for their weapons. He was counting on Nantan to take care of the problem, but if these men were trigger happy and ready to shoot on sight, then he was an easy target for them. The reaction he wanted was the one he got though. Both men leveled their rifles in his direction, but they could clearly see that he had one of their own with him. Eric slowly raised his hands, so that they could see they were empty.

"Tell them!" He whispered, without looking at the prisoner. "Don't get it wrong!"

"DON'T SHOOT! We ran into trouble on the road! This guy helped me out!"

Eric still had his hands up, but he was watching the two guards intently, trying to anticipate their reaction. They looked at each other for a second, one of them saying something he couldn't hear, and then the other shouted back, his order directed at Eric: "Keep your hands up where I can see them and stay where you are!" Even as he said it, the other man had turned and started back towards the nearest building that was visible in the compound. Eric didn't see anyone else outside in the parts of the yard that he could see from that vantage point, but he knew the second guy was about to alert everyone there that something was up. The one remaining at his post stood there with his rifle pointed at Eric, all of his attention focused on the unexpected visitor and his own comrade who'd left in a truck and returned riding a horse. And so it was that he didn't seem to notice when the other man behind him, who had taken several long strides in the opposite direction, suddenly stumbled and clutched at his neck, before collapsing onto the hard gravel surface of the yard.

Eric showed no reaction to this event that might tip off the one focused on him, but it wouldn't have mattered anyway, because just seconds after the first man fell, the other also dropped his rifle as his body went limp and gave way beneath him; Nantan's head shot killing him before he hit the ground. Wilson saw it all of course, and he was struggling against his bonds in desperation, but he didn't dare try to yell, so Eric wasn't concerned with him for now. Eric dismounted with his M4 in hand and quickly led the two horses into the brush beside the road, where he tied them off. A quick scan of the compound when he emerged revealed no indication their arrival had been noticed yet, and Nantan came out to help him drag the bodies out of sight.

The suppressed .22 caliber rifle had done its job, and no one in the compound seemed to have heard it. Eric figured the rest of the men were inside the two main buildings, one of which looked like the office, with the radio tower standing tall nearby, and the other a large metal-roofed workshop area and garage, where the forest service had maintained their equipment and vehicles. If what Wilson had told them was the truth, there were only six men remaining there, including the chief, since the men of the escort detail and gate security made up more than half of the total number working from this post at the present time. That seemed about right to Eric, knowing what he did of such operations, but he wasn't taking Wilson at his word and was ready for anything as he and Nantan quickly crossed the yard to the nearest wall of the office building. Red remained hidden near the perimeter, covering them with his rifle. He was in pain, but he'd insisted on doing his part, saying it wouldn't affect his ability to shoot. Luke and Tommy were in position to provide crossfire from the opposite direction, so Eric focused on his main goal of gaining control of the radio and persuading the chief to use it to call the men of the escort detail.

He and Nantan had just taken up positions on either side of the wooden porch across the front of the office building when the main door opened. Both of them ducked below the level of the deck and Nantan raised the Ruger to take the man out once he'd stepped down to the ground, but Eric shook his head and gave him a signal to hold off. For all he knew, whoever was coming out could be the chief, and even if he wasn't, Eric needed a new hostage on the inside of the compound to use for leverage. The doorway to this building was angled in a way that anyone coming out couldn't immediately see the front perimeter gate, so Eric knew the man wouldn't realize anything was wrong until he descended the four steps to the yard, and then only if he happened to glance that way. Eric signaled to Nantan again to watch the door in case someone else followed him out, and then he placed his M4 on the ground beside him and prepared to spring. From the bottom step to where he was crouched was less than ten feet, so when his adversary's foot touched the gravel, Eric had already launched himself for the tackle. His body weight slammed the man into the ground with enough force to knock the wind out of him, and Eric followed up with two vicious blows to the face with his fists, further stunning him before he had a chance to cry out or react. Eric pulled him under the edge of the deck and out of sight, checking him for weapons before doing anything else. He found a full-sized pistol in a thigh holster on his right leg, and quickly yanked it away and tossed it farther under the deck, before pushing the muzzle of his own Glock into the man's temple and leaning over so that he could talk to him in a low voice.

"One word and a round goes through your brain, got it? Don't answer, just nod your head!"

The man did, and Eric continued. "I'm looking for the man you call 'chief', the one who's in charge here. Is that you, or is he inside this building?"

The man turned his eyes away, saying nothing, and before Eric could offer him more persuasion, he was stopped short by the sound of the door opening again. This time, whoever was coming outside seemed to be in a hurry, storming across the deck and yelling for someone named 'Mullins.' Eric knew it was the one he'd taken down when his captive completely ignored his directive and called back to his boss: "CHIEF!"

It was the last word he uttered before Eric silenced him with a hammer blow to the temple from the butt of his Glock, but it was more than enough to set into motion the sequence of events that would wrap up the action in the compound. First, there was the shout from Nantan, ordering the other man on the porch to freeze. But by the time Eric was able to look, Nantan was firing towards the door with the suppressed .22 and Eric heard it slam shut as the chief retreated inside. Seconds later, bullets tore through the wooden door from within and Eric and Nantan flattened themselves against the walls on either side.

"Did you hit him?" Eric called to Nantan.

"Yes, at least once in the upper leg. I was trying to take him down without killing him."

"Good! That'll keep him inside." Eric knew the sounds of the chief's gunshots would draw the attention of the others, who were likely in the work building, and it was best to let those who responded believe the only threat was here, where their leader was pinned down in his office. He stuck his head around the corner to look, and sure enough, saw men with rifles rushing outside to see what was going on. Eric fired a couple of rounds in their direction just to keep them interested, knowing that he was putting all his faith in Tommy and Luke to take care of this from the other side. And if any got through, they still had Red out there watching from near the front gate.

The men who were advancing on him were professionals, and once they understood there was a real threat at the office building, there was no hasty or heroic charge to come to the aid of their boss. They were no doubt working out a plan to flank him and take him out, but what they hadn't counted on was that they were the ones walking into the trap, rather than closing one of their own. Eric heard the reports from beyond the perimeter as Tommy and Luke opened fire. They were shooting in semi-auto mode, but at a fairly rapid rate of fire between the two of them. Eric then heard Red's rifle from out front and figured at least one of the contractors had tried to escape the crossfire from the rear and had exposed himself to Red. It was clearly a slaughter back there in the compound yard behind the office building, but Eric and Nantan could see none of it from where they waited. The shooting was intense and seemed to go on for a long time, but Eric knew that the perception of time in a firefight was often different than the reality, and that the whole thing was probably less than a minute. He and Nantan waited much longer, just to be sure though, and there was still the matter of the chief, who was armed and still alive inside the office. When Nantan's men moved in after sweeping the rest of the compound to check for resistance, they assured him all was clear. They had the office surrounded, but Eric had no time for, nor was he in the mood for, a standoff.

"You can surrender now, and live, or we'll just throw a grenade through the window and be done with this. Your choice!" Eric called out to him. There was no immediate reply, so he followed up. Eric and the Apaches had no grenades, and of course he didn't want to take the guy out just yet anyway, because he thought it best if the radio call to the men in the escort came directly from their boss, rather than a stranger they would disregard. "My men and I have you surrounded, and all of your security neutralized, including the crew of the truck returning from the road. We know who you're working for, but I'm not concerned with that part of your operation. Three or four days ago though, you raided a cabin in the mountains to the southeast of here and took a woman captive. We know she left here this morning in one of the vehicles your men were escorting. All we want is that convoy stopped."

"Why would I do that? You've killed my men, and you'll kill me too!"

"The answer is simple. If you do nothing, we kill you right now. If you cooperate, we take you with us to wherever those trucks are stopped, and if the woman is there and unhurt, then you and your other men are free to go. I've stated my offer, and you have thirty seconds to decide. My stopwatch is running!"

Eric was confident the chief would accept his offer. To get where he was in this outfit, Eric knew the man was loyal to no one and accustomed to working for the highest bidder. This time, the price was his life, and his entire team in the compound had just been wiped out in a matter of minutes. The man knew a deal when he saw one, and before those thirty seconds ticked away, Eric had his answer.

"Okay! Hold up! I surrender!"

"Open the door slowly and come out with your hands on top of your head. You know the drill, Chief!"

Eric and Nantan stood waiting with their rifles aimed at the door. Nantan's other men stood by from a safer distance in case something went wrong. But the door opened as directed, and the chief stepped out, limping. Blood had soaked through the right leg of his pants all the way down to his boot, but the chief had wrapped several turns of duct tape around the wound in his upper thigh to slow the flow and seemed unfazed by the pain as he stood there facing his captors. He was a wiry middle-aged man with sandy blonde hair and a clean-shaven face that bore a long scar across his left cheek and jaw, and he stared back at Eric and Nantan, sizing them up as they waited for him to speak.

"So, who is this woman and what is so important about her that you have gone to all this trouble and killed good men to get her back?"

"She's my wife!" Eric said. "That's what!"

Fourteen

SHAUNA WAS SO COLD in the unheated supply room where they'd locked her up that she was unable to sleep at night. The man who brought her food, water and a bucket to serve as a toilet had also given her a single wool blanket, but even wrapped tightly in that, she was far too cold when the temperatures plunged after dark. She found stacks of invoices, purchase orders and catalogs on the shelves left there from when the forest service had been using the place and spread them on the bare concrete floors to create some insulation, but it still wasn't enough. That first night was excruciating, because she'd had no more contact with the chief or anyone else that would talk to her, and she had no idea how long it would be until they turned her over to the Army, like he said they would. She didn't want to end up in one of the refugee camps, but anything was better than this, or so it seemed at the time. But as she lay there shivering in the cold, she couldn't help but think Jonathan and Vicky were worse off than she. How were they going to survive up on that mountain without the shelter of the cabin or even the barn? It still didn't make sense to her that they would have gone far enough away to be unaware of what was happening there, or to hear the automatic rifle fire when she was captured by the men chasing her. The only thing Shauna could think of was that perhaps they *had* seen and heard it all and had wisely remained hidden out of sight. She hoped that was the case, and that they really did have Tucker with them, since he was missing from among the other horses. Thinking about the poor animals that were shot gave Shauna a sick feeling inside. What kind of man was this 'chief' to order such a thing? The kind she couldn't trust, she knew that, and the more time went by without hearing from him, the more she began to doubt he was going to do what he said he would and take her to the authorities. And if he didn't do that, then what *did* he have in mind for her? Shauna didn't know, but she was determined to fight to the end if it came to that.

By the morning of the third day of confinement in that isolated room, Shauna was kicking the walls and dumping parts and supplies out of their boxes in her rage. She pulled herself up to the sill of the tiny window and screamed out into the compound for the chief, but if anyone heard her, they ignored it. The only thing that broke the monotony and finally brought the man in charge out where she could hear his voice again was the arrival of vehicles later that afternoon, just before dark. Shauna heard them pulling into the compound, and then the slamming doors and greetings and introductions among the men. She heard a voice she thought was the chief's speaking to whoever had arrived in English, and then switching to Spanish. Shauna couldn't follow all of it, but it sounded like one of the guests was speaking congratulatory words regarding the success of some operation, and from the direction the conversation was going, everyone seemed to be in good cheer.

Shauna yelled through the window to the chief while she knew he could hear her, and the voices stopped for a few seconds before the men began laughing and then talking about her in Spanish. She could hear the chief describing her in terms that were completely inappropriate, and she decided she'd best stay quiet and hope their attention would revert back to whatever they'd been talking about before. Later that evening, after dark, the compound came alive with music and laughter, and Shauna could tell the chief's men were drinking and partying with their guests. She backed against the opposite wall when she heard the padlock click open on the outside of her door, but the man that entered was the same guy that had been bringing her food since they brought her there.

"Enjoy your dinner! You're getting out of here tomorrow, so it'll be the last time you'll get our chow!" He put her plate down and backed out to close the door.

"Wait! What's going on? Am I going to be taken to a military post like the chief said?"

"No idea! You'll have to ask him in the morning," The man said, before slamming the door behind him.

The noise outside grew louder later into the night, and Shauna was afraid to even try to sleep for fear someone else would unlock her door. She paced the floor and waited, shivering against the wall in her blanket until well after midnight, when the ruckus finally died down. Morning came, and she dozed off a little, until they came for her about an hour and a half after sunrise. Two of the men from the team that had raided the cabin entered the room and took her by the arm on either side before leading her out into the gravel yard in the middle of the compound. Shauna saw the chief standing there with some of his other men and five hard-looking Hispanic guys who appeared to be as combat ready as the contractors. Behind them were two black GMC SUVs, and two of the same crew cab pickups that had been waiting at the place where the men had switched from horses to trucks the day they captured her.

"Your ride is here," Chief said. "Sorry we couldn't offer you better accommodations while you were with us, but I'm sure there'll be better days ahead for you."

"What is this? You said you were taking me to a military base. I'm not going anywhere with those men!"

"It's the best I can do, given the circumstances. We've had issues come up that we have to attend to. My friend,

Pascual, will see to it that you are taken to a safer place, and I'll bet the food will be a lot better than here too."

"No wait! I'll stay here! I don't mind! I'll wait until you have contact again with a regular Army patrol or whatever. I have to talk to someone that can help me find my husband and daughter!"

"I'm sorry, lady, but I can't keep you here any longer. Please, just get in the vehicle. You'll be okay."

Shauna tried to pull away from the two that were holding her, but they were both strong men with grips like iron. They lifted her bodily from the ground by the arms and carried her to the second SUV, where one of the Hispanic men was standing with the back door open. Shauna kicked at that man and the legs of the two that were holding her, but the three of them forced her into the back seat and then one of the two contractors holding her passed the Hispanic man a zip tie that he used to secure her right wrist to the grab handle above the inside of the door. This done, he slammed the door shut. Shauna twisted around on the seat to get into position where she could use her feet to kick at the window on the opposite side, but before she could break the glass, the same man opened that side and got in, forcing her back into her seat.

"*Tranquillo! Tranquillo, Señora!* We aren't going to hurt you. We are only giving you a ride."

"Where are you taking me? I have to get to an Army base or a refugee facility, so I can talk to someone that can help me!"

"It's okay! El jefe has told us everything. Just relax."

Shauna didn't believe this for a minute, but she knew it was a waste of energy to keep struggling right now. All she could do was wait for a better opportunity to escape, if such an opportunity ever came. Two more of the Hispanic men got into the front seat and the other two got into the other Yukon. The two pickups were apparently there to escort them out, and when they cleared the gates of the compound, the gray one was in the lead of the convoy, while the silver one brought up the rear, three men in each truck. Shauna had no idea where they were taking her, whether to another operating base they had in the region or somewhere beyond. As she pondered this, it suddenly occurred to her that they might even be headed to Mexico! Shauna had felt helpless many times since the events that started with the beginning of summer, but never so helpless as this.

She tried asking questions of the man in the seat beside her, but now he pretended not to understand English, and when she switched to her limited Spanish, he simply ignored her. Shauna gave up and resigned herself to the fact that she was going to have to wait until they reached wherever they were going and hope there would be someone there with whom she could reason. In the meantime, she resolved to take careful note of the route they were driving, as she had no idea how far they would travel. There was only one way out of the compound at the end of the gravel road, so that part was easy. But when they reached the pavement, the trucks didn't turn left and head back to the east the way she'd been brought here. Instead they took a right and headed west. Shauna also noted that while the pickup truck in front continued to lead the way, the one following them turned around in the intersection and headed back in the direction of the compound.

Now that they were on the pavement and traveling faster, Shauna turned again to the man beside her, pointing to her wrist that was zip tied to the grab handle as she tried to find the right words in Spanish to explain that it was too tight. She had deliberately twisted and pulled against the restraint in advance, so that her fingers were turning blue and it appeared that her circulation was being cut off. *"Por favor!"* she pleaded.

There was a rapid-fire exchange in Spanish between the man beside her and the others up front. Shauna understood enough of it to know that one was against the idea of cutting her loose, but the guy in the back said he would watch her, and besides, she wouldn't jump out now because they were going too fast. After a couple more expletives that Shauna understood perfectly, the one up front in the passenger seat relented, and her seat mate pulled out a big folding knife and snapped the blade open with a flick of his wrist. Then he leaned forward and held the stiletto-like tip close in front of her eyes, whispering a warning that was easy to translate, regardless of the language barrier. Shauna nodded that she understood, and then thanked him when he slipped the blade into the tight space between her wrist and the grab handle and sliced away the thick plastic tie.

She certainly had no intention of jumping out of a moving vehicle but having both hands free made Shauna feel a lot better about her situation, even if there was little hope of escape. She couldn't just hop out and run, even when the vehicles came to a stop, because like the contractors, these men in the two SUVs were heavily armed. Shauna couldn't miss the two AK-47s leaning against the front seat by the console when they put her into the vehicle, and the man sitting next to her wore a pistol in a shoulder holster that was in plain sight under his unbuttoned coat. She figured the other two were carrying pistols as well, and then there were the three contractors in front of them and the two Mexicans in the other SUV bringing up the rear. No, running wouldn't work, unless something changed, and sometime about an hour after they'd first turned onto the pavement, it did.

The first indication she got that something was up came when the driver suddenly slowed and then stopped in the middle of the road. Shauna looked out the windows to see why but didn't think it was because they had arrived anywhere. The terrain here was much lower in elevation and she'd noticed the changing landscape and vegetation along the way after they'd slowly made their way out of the mountains on a steep, winding road. Here it looked almost like semi-desert, the low, rolling hills covered in dry brush and grasses. It seemed like an unusual place to stop, and from what she could understand of the conversation in her vehicle, the Mexicans were as confused as she.

She saw two of the contractors get out of the pickup truck with their rifles in their hands. One of the two remained in place next to their vehicle while the other approached the driver of hers. A conversation ensued that quickly turned into a heated argument. There was something said about having to wait there because the chief had forgotten something, and it would only be an hour or so. Shauna could tell the Mexicans didn't like this new development. The guy in the passenger's seat in front of her got out with one of the AKs in hand, yelling back at the two contractors, who insisted that they had to do this. Shauna then saw the third man exit the pickup with his rifle, and it was clear that it was becoming a standoff. She'd momentarily forgotten about the other SUV behind her when gunfire suddenly erupted, and all hell broke loose.

Shauna saw the contractors up front retreating for the cover of their truck as they brought their own weapons up to fire. The man who'd gotten out of the seat in front of her with the AK went down, and when the one beside her exited the vehicle with his pistol, Shauna saw him get hit and fall too. Bullets shattered the windshield on the driver's side as the last man inside dove to the floorboards for cover, and Shauna opened her door, deciding it was more dangerous to stay inside than to get out. The other two Mexicans in the rear SUV were still firing, so the battle wasn't over. Shauna knew it was now or never, so she dropped low into a crouch beside the door as she climbed out. She spotted the fallen AK where it lay on the shoulder of the road near the twitching body of the man who'd carried it and scooped it up as she broke into a sprint for the brush. Keeping as low as she possibly could, she busted through thorny branches that ripped at her hands and clothing, but she never looked back. It didn't matter to her who won and who lost the unexpected firefight, she knew her only chance was to get away from both parties, so she didn't pause until she was completely out of sight of the road. She checked the chamber of the AK and pulled the magazine out to verify that it was full. The weapon was the real deal, and not a civilian clone, and the selector switch was in the full auto position when she'd grabbed it. Shauna switched it to safe and kept going, keeping her finger near the lever and ready if she needed to fire.

The shooting behind her stopped as suddenly as it had begun though, and Shauna heard cursing in English that told her it was the chief's men that had prevailed. Why this had happened, she had no idea, but now one of the men was calling out to her, saying that it was safe to come back and that the danger was over. She heard him yell to her that they were in the middle of nowhere, and that she would die out here if left alone, but Shauna ignored him and kept going. She didn't know if they would come after her or not, but if they did, she was determined they weren't going to take her captive again. She set out at a run, working her way around the worst of the thickets and among the rocks as the terrain climbed the farther she got from the road. It was almost like Déjà vu from just a few days ago, but in a different setting. This wasn't going to be like the last time she ran from these men though. She wasn't trying to create a diversion today; she was running for her life. This time she knew for sure that they weren't U.S. soldiers, she knew what they were capable of, and she was armed with an AK-47 rifle and she had a good head start. But when their calls for her to stop didn't seem to be receding into the distance as she ran, Shauna knew the contractors were coming after her. She scanned the terrain above her looking for cover that would give her an advantage, and when she found it among a jumble of large boulders, Shauna took up position there and switched the selector on her weapon back to full auto. It was several more minutes before the first man came into view 150 yards below, and Shauna didn't know if all three of them had survived the firefight with the Mexicans or not and didn't care. If she could eliminate one of them now it would improve her odds regardless. She squeezed the trigger without hesitation, easing her finger off only when the muzzle began to climb. It was maybe a five or six round burst, but it was enough. She saw the man go down, and it wasn't an intentional dive for cover either. He folded up at the waist and dropped, either dead or wounded. Shauna waited a few minutes to see if the other two would appear, but when they didn't, she got to her feet and took off running again, thinking that maybe the others had decided she wasn't worth it. Perhaps they didn't see her grab the AK and had no idea she was armed until she fired.

She ran fast, driven by adrenalin and the pent-up energy from all that time confined in the little supply room. The afternoon air was already chilly, and she knew the night would bring real cold, but right now the important thing was putting distance between herself and the road. She had no idea where she was or how big this tract of desolate land into which she was fleeing might be, but she thought that if she could just elude them until dark and find a place to survive the night, she would figure out the rest tomorrow.

Fifteen

ERIC, NANTAN AND LUKE stood around the desk where the base station radio unit was set up and watched as the chief attempted to make the call to his men in the escort truck. He repeated his contact attempt several times before he got a reply.

"Yes, Reece, you heard me right. Stop the trucks! I don't care what you tell the Mexicans. Tell them I forgot something else I had for them, and that I'm bringing it to them. Just make sure the woman doesn't go anywhere and give me a call back as soon as you have it all under control."

The chief turned to Eric, "They'll get it done. Juan Lopez isn't going to like it, but Reece knows how to bullshit him into waiting. We don't need to keep them waiting too long though, or they'll start getting nervous."

Eric looked at the map the chief had sketched on a piece of paper, showing the route the convoy took and the approximate location of where they were when his man answered the call. Despite the amount of time that had passed, much of the route was slow and tedious on mountain roads, so they weren't that far away. "I've changed my mind about taking you with us, Chief." Eric turned to Tommy and Luke. "We'll go in two vehicles. Check the fuel levels and get them out to the gate. Get that other guy, Wilson, off the horse and bring him in the compound."

"If you say so, but why not just shoot him? We don't need him."

"Because I told him I wouldn't if he gave me the correct information about his boss here, so I won't."

"Wilson?" The chief spat. "That son of a bitch gave you all that? No wonder you took us down as easy as you did. You ought to kill him, because if you don't and you don't kill me, I'll damned sure do it myself!"

"That's between you and him, and you'll get your chance, but I would have taken you down with or without him."

"So that woman really is your wife, huh? I guess what she told me was true; that she had a real badass for a husband and that you were in the soldier-for-hire business too, but you came back here looking for your daughter. Good luck with that, man! I mean, I'd hate to know I had a daughter missing out here, the way things are going in this country."

"She's not missing anymore, but even if she was, I wouldn't stop until I found her, just like I won't stop until I take her mother back to her."

"And what about after that? Who are you working for? A guy like you has got to be working for somebody. What about your buddies here? They're not Mexican, but they're not white either. Indian?"

"Jicarilla Apache!" Nantan said. "We work for no one!"

"And I'm officially retired," Eric said. "I'd suggest you do the same after today. Your illicit operations with the drug cartels are about to come to an end."

Eric made the chief show him where he'd been keeping Shauna detained, and when he saw the room, Eric shoved the man inside. "Put the other one in here too, and lock the door," he told Luke. "They can work out their differences in private while we're away."

"We have to come back for the horses, you know."

"Of course. In the meantime, they'll be fine with the run of the compound. I don't expect that we'll be gone all that long."

They drove the Land Rover and a pickup out of the compound and Tommy locked the gate behind them. Eric was at the wheel of the Land Rover with Nantan riding with him, while Luke, Tommy and Red followed in the truck. Since the chief had believed at the time that he was going with them as a hostage, Eric was confident that the route he'd sketched out for them was the correct one, and there had been no real need to bring him once he had that. His other three men in the escort truck thought their boss was coming to meet them where they stopped the Mexicans, so they would have their guard down when they saw the familiar

Land Rover and pickup roll up to where they were waiting. Eric hoped the element of surprise would enable him and the Apaches to take control of the situation without a fight, because the last thing he wanted was to have bullets flying while Shauna was in one of the vehicles.

They sped down the gravel road past the shot-up truck they'd ambushed earlier, leaving behind them a cloud of dust. Once on the pavement, Eric pushed it harder, knowing that like the chief said, the cartel guys that had Shauna weren't going to be happy about the unexpected delay, and were likely to get nervous if too much time passed. There hadn't been time to ask many questions, but Eric learned enough to know that the two SUVs had come there to make a delivery of cartel merchandise they were stockpiling for later when they expected the market to return. The chief was sending Shauna back with them because it was a convenient way to get her off his hands, and the Mexicans had agreed to it, saying their boss in Sonora had a thing for American blondes. Eric could only hope the men didn't try anything with her while they had her in the truck, which was another reason to intercept them with as little delay as possible.

The route led west winding through more mountains before it entered the more open country of lower elevations. Much of the landscape along the roadway was uninhabited rangeland, but here and there they passed the rubble of burned down ranch houses, and Eric figured that was the work of the C.R.I. contractors or the cartels. They really had taken control of the region and he was sure that the chief's operation was just a small part of the big picture. Eric was just wondering whether or not they might encounter other members of either group when he and Nantan spotted an approaching vehicle in the distance on the road ahead, coming their way at high speed.

"I'm pulling over to the shoulder," Eric said. "We'll see if they recognize the trucks and stop. It could be another C.R.I. patrol, so get ready!" Eric pressed the buttons to open both front windows of the Land Rover and waved back at Luke to follow him as he brought it to a stop. The oncoming truck was closing fast, and Eric knew the driver had seen them.

"It looks like the other truck we saw this morning," Nantan said. "The gray Ford."

"I think you're right, and if it is, they didn't wait like the chief told them to. Shauna may be with them, so we've got to keep our cool. There's no telling what they'll do when they see we're not who they think we are."

"I'll cover you from the rear," Nantan said, as he slipped out the door and closed it behind him.

"Tell the other guys to be ready!"

The approaching truck slowed as it came straight towards Eric, and he could see two men in the front. He was sure now that it was indeed the truck they'd seen escorting the black SUVs that morning, and the driver was pulling up to the Land Rover now, probably expecting to find the chief sitting there waiting. Eric saw the surprise on his face when he saw it was a stranger behind the wheel instead, and by then Nantan had stepped out from behind the vehicle with his rifle leveled on them. The man at the wheel threw the truck into reverse immediately and stomped the accelerator, backing away in an erratic weave as he tried to escape. Nantan opened fire, aiming at the tires, and when the truck came to a stop again with its front tires flattened, the guy in the passenger's seat began firing back at them, forcing Nantan back into cover and Eric to get down to the floorboards and crawl out the opposite door. *Dammit!* He cursed under his breath. He hadn't expected those idiots to try something like that with Nantan's rifle on them. Now they were under fire and couldn't really shoot back with purpose because they didn't know if Shauna was in that truck or not.

"We're going to have to flank them!" Eric said. "That truck's not going anywhere. If we can keep them focused on the Land Rover, it shouldn't be too hard."

"Let me and Luke do it. We'll go from either side of the road. Just keep shooting in their general direction so they don't get suspicious. Give us ten minutes."

"Tell Red to get that pickup back up the road, out of rifle range. If they disable both of our vehicles out here, we're screwed! If Tommy wants to help me keep them busy, that's up to him."

Nantan said he would, and Eric fired several more rounds in the direction of the two in the other truck. If it weren't for Shauna likely being in there, it would be a simple matter to take them out. As it was, it would still be simple, but it was going to take time for Nantan and Luke to get into place. In the meantime, Eric expected to take a lot of fire on the Land Rover, and he was correct in assuming it would be disabled when the two shooters directed their fire at the tires and the radiator, even as Red hurried out of range with the pickup. Tommy came into position alongside Eric by keeping low in the roadside ditch, and Eric made a dive for it to join him, deciding there was too much incoming fire to risk relying on just the vehicle for cover.

"They apparently aren't short on ammo, are they?" Eric said, as he took up position in the ditch near Tommy. Eric couldn't imagine what Shauna must be going through, if she were indeed in the back seat of that truck. She would have no idea who her captors were engaging, and she certainly would never imagine it was him. He knew she would know to keep down and stay put if at all possible, but it would still be a hair-raising situation for her, trapped there in the middle of a hot firefight. Eric and Tommy kept up their sporadic shooting to keep the two guys focused, but he knew they were experienced operators and that they would have to know they couldn't hold their position long against several armed men. If they suspected they were being flanked though, there was little they could do about it, because Nantan and Luke were so stealthy in their approach that neither was detected until it was too late. Eric heard their rifles as the two of them unleashed a simultaneous crossfire on the men behind the truck, and when the echoes faded away, there were no more sounds of resistance from that direction. Eric saw Nantan move in while Luke waited in place to cover him. A few seconds later, Nantan waved the all-clear signal, and Eric sprang to his feet and ran to the truck, hoping that Shauna was unhurt. But when he opened the back door and looked inside, there was no one there!

"Well crap! She's not here! Are both of those guys dead?"

Nantan nodded.

"Then we've got to get to the place where they turned around. Maybe they were unable to stop the Mexicans!" Eric said, as he waved frantically for Red to come forward with the other pickup. When he did, Eric took the wheel and they all piled into the truck. He drove as fast as the road would permit, his mind racing even faster as he thought of all the reasons why Shauna wasn't in that truck. The most likely one of all was the one he feared most—that the contractors escorting the Mexicans had been unable to stop them and even now they were driving away with her to no telling where. Eric knew there were originally three men in the truck, and he wondered if the other one had been killed when they tried to follow the chief's orders. He was so convinced that he was right about this that it came as quite a shock to find the two black SUVs stopped in the middle of the road, bodies sprawled all around them. Eric skidded to a stop from a safe distance and he and the Apaches got out, their rifles at ready. Nothing was moving in the vicinity, however, so they cautiously closed in on the bullet-riddled vehicles and checked the bodies, finding five Hispanic-looking men in total, all of them dead from bullet wounds. Some of their weapons were still laying there on the ground where they dropped them, and the men began picking them up while Eric examined the interiors of the SUVs, dreading what he might find there. There were no more bodies inside though, and the only evidence he found that Shauna had been there was a cut zip tie on one of the rear floorboards. Eric took it to Luke and asked him what he made of it.

"Well, she wasn't in the pickup with the two contractors, and she's not here, but one of those guys is missing too, so they must be nearby."

"I wonder why the other two would have headed back, when they'd already taken these cartel guys out and they thought the chief was coming here to meet them?"

"Your wife may have escaped. Maybe the other guy even helped her? Who knows? If they went on foot though, I'll find them. I'll start looking for their trail right now!"

Eric had full faith in Luke's tracking abilities after seeing them in action, and he wasn't let down now. Luke found the place where Shauna left the road, almost directly adjacent to the SUV in which Eric found the cut restraint. There was nothing else at the scene of the shootout to investigate, so Nantan asked Tommy and Red to stay behind and guard the truck while he and Eric followed Luke into the bush.

"She went through here. Three men went this way too," Luke pointed out the footprints where they crossed a sandy area among the rocks. "Two of them turned around and came back. The other one must be the third man who is missing."

Eric looked at the confusing jumble of tracks in the sand, many of them obscured by the newer ones on top of them. "So, they all went after her at first. Can you tell how far ahead she was?"

"Not exactly, but she was running faster than them, making longer strides. They were in a hurry too, but they stopped several times, probably trying to figure out where she was. But then, when the two of them came back this way, they were only walking. See their boot prints over the top of the others? Those two had to be the two in the truck we met on the road. But the other one may be still following her. We need to move quickly, but with caution too, because he is out there somewhere."

Eric was impressed that Luke could tell all that, but not really surprised. He knew the basics of how to read sign, but what separated his elemental knowledge from a master like

Luke was that Luke could follow a trail through places where most people couldn't tell it even existed. That was a skill that took years of study and Eric hadn't had the patience or the time, but he was glad that Luke did. Without him, Eric would be mostly guessing, perhaps finding a foot print here and there, but stumbling around blind trying to figure out where Shauna went until it was possibly too late to help her.

It seemed strange to Eric that the other two would turn back and leave just the one guy in pursuit, but he thought that maybe it was because they realized by the way she was running that catching her wasn't going to be quick and easy. Perhaps they left their most skilled tracker to it while the others went back to get help. But that theory proved wrong when Luke had followed the trail but another quarter mile. The third man was face down and unmoving on the blood-stained rocks beneath him, and a closer look revealed two bullet exit wounds in the middle of his back.

"That is why only two of them went back," Luke smiled.

"Your wife must have grabbed a weapon before she ran," Nantan said. "The other two must have decided she wasn't worth the bother."

Eric agreed that might be right. They'd just survived a major firefight with the men who they were supposed to be working for, killing them all, and this woman the chief had already traded off or given to those men as a gift had then killed one of their own while escaping into the wilderness.

Eric could see why they'd have little motivation to continue pursuit. They were hired killers when killing was the job, but no one was paying them any extra to risk their lives going after some crazy bitch they had no use for anyway, so they'd collected their dead buddy's weapon and headed back to their truck.

Luke pointed out where Shauna's trail was headed, and Eric scanned the slopes in that direction and easily picked out the logical spot from which she would have set up her ambush. When the three of them reached the jumble of boulders, Luke found several 7.62 x 39mm shell casings on the ground there. "Looks like she's got an AK," he grinned. "That's good shooting, considering the weapon and the distance."

"She knows how to handle a rifle," Eric agreed. He felt much better now, knowing Shauna was armed, but when Luke picked up her trail where she'd continued on after firing her weapon, her footprints indicated she left at a fast run. There was no telling how many miles that woman would cover before dark if she thought for a minute she was still being pursued. Eric was no slouch at distance running himself, but even if he knew her exact route, Shauna had a good head start. Since he didn't know though, there was no way he'd ever catch up without Luke's help. "You may as well go back and tell Tommy and Red we're going to be awhile," Eric told Nantan. "My ex-wife is a freakin' triathlete and may run all night. If Luke is willing, the two of us will go after her until we catch up."

Sixteen

WHEN SHE REACHED THE top of the ridge above the place where she'd stopped to fire at her pursuers, Shauna saw that the only way ahead was across a wide plain that stretched to another range of hazy blue peaks in the far distance. Bisecting the flatlands ahead of her though was what appeared to be a deep canyon. She couldn't tell from where she stood if there was a way across it or not, but she picked a spot where it looked like a shallow arroyo on her side intersected it. If she could make it down there, she knew she might find a way into the canyon, which she hoped would offer better places to shelter and hide and maybe even a source of water.

Aside from getting shot or captured by her pursuers, finding water was right up there in importance with finding shelter from the cold. Shauna was confident in her endurance and ability to run for miles and miles without stopping, but without water the dry climate here would do her in after all that exertion. She was putting all her faith in being able to find some in the deep rift ahead of her, because to remain where she was would surely result in her capture. Dodging rocks and picking her way through the brush, Shauna made her way down to the plain at a fast lope. The land there wasn't as open as it appeared from a distance, and she felt better as she ran among the stunted cedars and other semi-desert vegetation that hid her from view of the ridge behind. She only stopped to look back once, and that was when she'd finally reached the edge of the arroyo. What she saw back there kept her from pausing more than a few seconds though. Silhouetted in the late afternoon sun at the crest of the distant ridge, were the tiny figures of two men! *They weren't giving up! The remaining two contractors were apparently tracking her even though she'd left them that far behind!*

Shauna still had no idea why those men had stopped the convoy out there in the middle of nowhere. Was it some kind of trick the chief's men had pulled on the Mexicans, handing her over to them and then having his men turn on them and kill them once they were out on the road? It didn't make a lot of sense, because she figured they could have done the same in the compound, had they wanted, but whatever the reason, it had happened, and now those men apparently wanted her back. She'd thought that taking out one of them with the AK had changed their minds, but now she knew she was wrong. The other two were still in pursuit, even though they were traveling far slower. She figured she must have wounded, rather than killed the one she shot, and that maybe getting him back to the road and tending his wounds had cost them sufficient time for her to gain such a good lead on them. Whatever the reason, she intended to keep her distance, and that meant she couldn't slack up now. Shauna climbed down into the shallow arroyo and followed its winding course that she hoped would take her to the big canyon she'd seen from the ridge. The men behind her would have seen it too, but Shauna was counting on the vastness of the landscape to enable her to disappear. It was only a short time until dark, and if she could just stay ahead until then, she was confident she could elude them.

As she worked her way down the dry stream bed, Shauna was conscientious about where she placed her steps. If they were tracking her, they would look for the obvious, so she avoided the sand whenever possible and walked on the smooth surfaces of the rocks, taking care not to overturn them or leave other obvious signs of her passage. She'd hoped to find standing water somewhere in the bottom of the arroyo, but there was none so far. This area was far drier than any she'd seen in Colorado since she and Jason had reached the Front Range, and Shauna figured the weather systems that had already brought snow to the high mountains didn't affect this particular region. If there was water in the vicinity, it would be farther down, probably in the bottom of the main canyon. Shauna's hopes of getting some soon faded though when she came to the end of the arroyo and found herself on a precipice that dropped more than a hundred feet to the canyon floor below. She crept as close to the edge of the cliff as she dared and looked over. There was water there all right, big pools of it in the bends of the canyon in the shadows of its near-vertical walls. But there was no way down there from where she stood without a climbing rope with which to rappel, so Shauna turned back to find a way out of the arroyo and then make her way along the rim of the canyon to search for another route.

Doing this required her to backtrack nearly a quarter of a mile just to get out of the arroyo. Then she had to follow it back down from the top to return to the canyon. All this time, she had to assume her pursuers were gaining on her, but though she stopped to look back when possible, she saw no sign of them. The next place she saw that could be a potential way down was a narrow slot canyon she came to another mile farther along the rim. It was easy enough to enter from the top, but from up there she couldn't tell whether it was climbable all the way down or not. Shauna had seen the water in the main canyon floor though, so she was determined to try and reach it, and pressed ahead. In places, the slot was so narrow she had to turn her body sideways to get through. The winding passageway between the vertical walls of smooth sandstone was taking her lower down with every step, but she still wasn't sure if she could reach the bottom until it finally ended at a drop off that she estimated was fifteen feet above the still water below. Shauna got down on her belly and crawled to the edge to look over, hoping to spot some hand or foot holds by which she could climb the rest of the way down, but the rock beneath her was smooth and featureless.

Her throat was parched, and the deep water directly below looked cool and inviting, a pale turquoise green pool that was clear enough that she could see several feet into it. She thought it was deep enough to jump into from that height without risk of injury, but even at this hour, the floor of the canyon was completely in the shadows, the sun well behind the tall cliffs of the rim. Shauna was cold despite her exertion, and she knew if she plunged into that water, she'd have no way to get warm again before the coming night. She had nothing with which to make a fire and her clothes would be soaked. There was a sandbar on the opposite side of the deep pool, but it was too far away to reliably throw her clothes, boots and rifle to it, even if she decided to take the plunge naked and try to warm up afterwards. She knew that getting her clothing wet with no way to dry it could prove fatal, guaranteeing hypothermia when the temperatures dropped later that night, and she decided it wasn't worth the risk. It was a huge disappointment, but Shauna took one last look at that beautiful water and turned to retrace her route back up the slot canyon to the rim.

It was going to take everything she had, but Shauna was determined to find another way down to the bottom that wouldn't involve getting wet. She had just emerged from the slot canyon though when she spotted someone standing frozen behind a small bush. The man must have been following her and had stopped short when he saw her suddenly reappear. Shauna knew immediately that he wasn't one of the two contractors, but he was carrying an AR or M4-style rifle like them and wearing a Desert Tan boonie hat. Beneath the hat, his hair was long, framing a dark face she knew was Indian or Mexican. Shauna had no idea where he'd come from, and since she'd been climbing, the AK was slung behind her back and not at hand, so she spun around and darted back down into the slot canyon just as the man shouted out a greeting to her: "HEY! WAIT, DON'T RUN!"

She knew she had just two choices now. She could hide and ambush the stranger if he continued to follow her, or she could jump into that cold water that waited below and try to escape into the canyon. She decided on the latter, as she had no idea whether or not the man was alone. With no further hesitation, she entered the narrow section of the slot and had just disappeared when another voice stopped her short: "SHAUNA! HEY SHAUNA... IT'S ME! ERIC...!"

The voice was distorted as it echoed off the wall of the canyon. Shauna had given the chief Eric's name when she was trying to convince him who she was and why she was there at Bob Barham's cabin. It was possible the men pursuing her were trying to trick her, but how did that explain the strange man she'd just seen? The one that looked Native

American? She wanted to believe that it really was Eric up there calling to her by some miracle, but how in the hell would *he* have known to look for her here?"

"SHAUNA! You can stop now! You're safe and Megan is too! I found her!"

Shauna felt her knees go weak as she leaned against the wall of the canyon and listened to the echo of those words. *Could this be real?* She heard Eric call out again, telling her that the men chasing her were dead, and then Shauna turned and climbed up through the bend she'd just rounded. When she came into view of the ledge above, two men were standing there: the stranger she'd just seen and Eric Branson! Shauna climbed the rest of the way out without another word. She was too exhausted to shout back and forth. When she reached the top, Eric was waiting and took her hands in his.

"You really found Megan? Where is she? Is she really okay? Is she here with you?"

"Yes, I found her, Shauna! She's safe and well! She's at the Jicarilla reservation, right where Vicky said she was going. She's there with her friend Aaron and his aunt and uncle."

"Are you sure she's okay there? Why did you leave her?"

"Yes, I'm sure, or I wouldn't have left her! And why do you think? To come back for you, of course! Just like I said I would in my letter."

Shauna had momentarily forgotten all about the letter. Now she remembered it and remembered how she'd cursed

Eric when she'd read it, and how she'd sworn that she was going to slap the hell out of him the next time she saw him. But she just looked at him through the tears of happiness welling up in her eyes and threw herself into his arms. *Megan was alive, and Eric Branson had found her, just like he said he would do!* She had so many questions, but for this moment, she just wanted to feel safe in his arms and grateful for all he'd done. When he finally pulled away, he introduced her to Luke, the tracker who'd made it possible to follow her here.

"We should get going," Luke said. "It will be dark now before we get back to the road. Nantan and the others are waiting, and we don't know that there aren't more of those guys patrolling these roads."

"Yeah, we've got a lot of miles to cover. I knew we were in for a workout when Luke said your tracks indicated you were running, Shauna. I guess if it hadn't been for this canyon, we'd be chasing you all night!"

Shauna told her story as the three of them set out for the hike back to the road. The first thing she told Eric, of course, was that she had no idea what had become of Jonathan and Vicky when the contractors raided the cabin. Then, Eric told her about Vicky's note, and how Wolf, the other experienced Jicarilla tracker they had with them, had gone after them.

"He will have no trouble catching up to them," Luke said. "They are traveling slow, because the girl is walking, while the injured guy rides on the only horse they have."

Shauna was relieved to know for sure that the two of them had indeed escaped discovery by the raiding party, and that Tucker was with them, the only horse on the place that escaped the senseless slaughter those horrible men had perpetrated. She was also happy to hear that most of the bastards were dead, including the other two that had been with the one she'd shot herself. But out of all of them, she thought it was the chief that deserved it the most.

"He's not going anywhere until we get back to the compound where we left our horses. Nantan has expressed an interest in talking further with him, so I will leave it up to him to do what is right. There are ways to get information out of men like that, and I'm quite sure there's a lot he can reveal about the extent of the cartel operations here and the involvement of this company he works for. If he cooperates with the Jicarilla, he may get a chance to tell it to the appropriate Army officials as well. But my part of this fight is over, unless we run into more trouble on the way back to the reservation."

Eric told Shauna that Megan had found help at an Army outpost on a highway to the east of the divide, and that was how she eventually reached the reservation. He said that after they were all safely back there again, he would attempt to make contact with the unit that assisted her and see if they might offer help or at least ideas as to how all of them could return to Louisiana. It was all so much for Shauna to take in that it seemed overwhelming as the two of them followed Luke back through the brush in the growing darkness. Just an hour earlier, she'd been running for her life with nothing remaining but her determination to avoid recapture. Now, it seemed that all was right with the world. Megan was found, and she was on her way to see her! And Eric was talking about Louisiana! That was a world so far away from her since she'd reached these mountains that she had given little thought to going back there or anywhere else as long as Megan was out here. Now it all came suddenly back to her. It seemed so strange to think that she had another family waiting for her back there; her husband, Daniel, and her stepson, Andrew. It wasn't that she'd forgotten about them, it was just that she'd put them out of her mind for the time being because they were safe there with Keith and Bart, while she was doing what she had to do here. Now though, she realized that everything was going to change again when she got back there, and she didn't know what to think about it. As mad as she'd been at Eric for leaving her at that cabin the way he did, it seemed so right to be with him at this moment, on their way together to be with their daughter. Shauna took Eric's hand as they walked, following Luke in the dark. It felt good to be close to Megan's father again, and Shauna didn't want it to end. And if the Apache tracker hadn't been there with them, there was no telling what might have happened right then and there in the desert.

Seventeen

JONATHAN DIDN'T HESITATE TO raise his hands when the voice out there in the dark commanded him to do so. It was accompanied by the unmistakable sound of a shotgun slide chambering a round, so Jonathan abandoned all thoughts of reaching for his own rifle, and he verified with a glance that Vicky's hands were up as well. He'd known every night when they built a fire that it was a security risk, but they had taken their chances, because without fire, the cold would be unbearable, and that evening, they had also needed it to cook the rabbit he'd shot. He'd thought they were far enough away from any of the roads and ranches they'd passed that day to make it unlikely anyone would spot a small campfire, but apparently, he was wrong. As he strained to see out into the darkness, Jonathan wondered what was about to happen to him and Vicky, and he felt like a helpless fool, sitting there with his hands in the air and a broken leg, unable to defend the beautiful young woman who'd done so much to help him.

"Don't move and nobody gets hurt," the voice spoke again.

By now, Jonathan could see something out there, and then, a man appeared at the edge of the ring of firelight, the hood of his jacket pulled over his head and a bandana covering his face below his eyes. Jonathan could see the shotgun pointed at them from where the man held it at waist level.

"What do you want from us? We don't have anything of value. If we're trespassing on your land or something, we didn't know, and we'll move on now."

"This isn't my land, and you're welcome to stay. I'll decide if you've got anything of value to me or not, but I'll start with that rifle you were about to reach for. And the horse."

"You can't take Tucker!" Vicky yelled back at him. "He's all we've got. My friend here is recovering from a broken leg, and he can't walk. Without the horse, he won't survive!"

"Not my problem," the stranger said. "I need that horse because I've got a long way to ride. I've got family counting on me to get back to them. Now both of you, get down flat on the ground, face down, and put your hands behind your heads where I can see them! Don't try anything stupid. I've been through enough lately, and I swear I'd just as soon blow your brains out as look at you!"

"Don't argue, Vicky!" Jonathan whispered to her. "We don't have much choice!"

Jonathan knew the man might shoot them anyway, but he had a pretty good feeling that he wouldn't if they complied and kept their mouths shut. It was going to suck to lose Tucker and the rifle and maybe everything else, but it could be far worse. His first thought when the stranger pointed the gun at them was that he was going to want Vicky, but now that didn't seem to be the case. Jonathan realized even as he got down to the ground that if the man had wanted to, he could have shot him dead from out there in the dark before they had a clue he was there, and then done what he wanted with her. Since he didn't, there was a glimmer of hope.

When he approached the fire, the man spotted the .44 Magnum on Vicky's belt, as she'd been unable to draw it or hide it when they were taken by surprise. Jonathan was almost relieved when the man pulled it from the holster, because he'd been afraid Vicky would try to go for it, especially upon learning that the man planned to take Tucker, and that would have probably gotten them shot.

"Nice big Magnum! You two were loaded for bear! I like it! Where'd you come from? Where are you headed?"

"What do you care?" Vicky spat. "You're just a thieving criminal!"

"No, I'm just a survivor. I'm no different than you. How do I know you didn't come by these guns and that horse the same way?" By now he had spotted the .22 Magnum carbine too, and he leaned it and the .45-70 lever gun against a rock a safe distance away. Then he carried their other belongings over there, so he could safely go through them while keeping an eye on them both.

"You're well-armed, but you don't have much else, do you? Tell you what, I'll split these energy bars and whatever this freeze-dried stuff is with you, and I'll take the horse and the two rifles. I'm going to unload this revolver and put the cartridges right back here with your stuff. When I ride out of here, I'll leave the revolver on top of that big rock over there," he pointed to a flat-topped boulder just visible at the edge of the light. I'll be gone before you can load it, but I'd better not see you move until I'm out of sight. I think it's a generous offer, considering, and you're welcome!"

"Who do you think you are?" Vicky screamed at him as the man lifted Tucker's saddle into place and began cinching it up. "There's no lower form of life than a horse thief! That horse belonged to my grandpa!"

"Don't waste your breath, Vicky!" Jonathan shushed her with a low whisper, trying to calm her down. "You're not going to talk him out of it. Just be glad he's not going to hurt us."

"But he is hurting us, Jonathan. He's leaving us out here in the wilderness to die!"

"We're not dead yet. We'll figure it out. Now don't push our luck. We need that .44 Magnum, so don't make him change his mind!"

Moments later, the stranger was mounted up and riding slowly back into the darkness. He stopped by the rock as promised and laid the revolver on the flat top. Then he spurred Tucker away and disappeared with one parting remark: "Good luck, folks!"

"Screw you, you asshole!" Vicky screamed, as she bolted up from the ground and ran to get the revolver. She didn't have the cartridges with her and Jonathan knew she wouldn't have fired at the man even if the gun was loaded, for fear of hitting Tucker. He fully understood how much this had to hurt her. Vicky loved Tucker and the two of them had a bond going back long before all this happened, when horses suddenly became of major importance again. And she was right that without him, they were indeed in deep trouble and were now truly in desperate survival mode. He had no idea what they would do next, but he knew it would be tough for him to get far out here without a horse, much less all the way to New Mexico.

Vicky came storming back over to the campfire, dropping to her knees to collect the cartridges for the .44 and load them into the cylinder of the big revolver. "I so wish I had just one clear shot at that guy. I would blow him away, Jonathan. I really would!"

"I know you would, Vicky, and I would to. I'm really sorry about Tucker. I know how much he meant to you."

"And you know how much we need him. What are we going to do, Jonathan?"

"I don't know, but we'll figure it out. I should have been ready for something like this. I should have had that rifle within easy reach at all times. I'm sorry, Vicky."

"It wouldn't have mattered. I had the .44 Magnum on me, but by the time I knew what was going on, he already had his gun pointed at us. I should have drawn it as soon as we knew something out there in the dark disturbed Tucker. It's as much my fault as yours. I guess we both got too complacent."

"Yeah, because we're way out here in the woods and it seems like we're well-hidden. Eric wouldn't have made that mistake, and I shouldn't have either, after what he tried to teach me."

"It's not going to do any good to dwell on what we should have done, Jonathan. We've got to focus on right now and figure out how to go forward."

"Yeah, that sounds exactly like something he'd say too. We can't do much tonight, but I think we need to find someplace else to wait it out until daylight. I don't trust that guy not to change his mind and come back here. And besides, if *he* saw our fire, someone else may have too."

"Good thinking. At least we don't have much to carry, and you do still have your crutch Bob made you. Come on,

I'll help you. I don't think we need to go far right now, just away from here a little."

Jonathan got to his feet on his on and using the crutch for support had no trouble standing and walking short distances, but to cut through the woods at night, he needed Vicky at his side for stability, and to prevent him from stumbling on something in the dark and perhaps breaking the other leg. He felt better about their security as soon as the darkness of the forest closed in around them. Despite losing so much, he knew he was lucky to be alive. The stranger could have simply shot him and taken Vicky if that had been what he wanted, so Jonathan felt they got off light, considering the alternatives.

There was no way they were going to risk building another fire, so their primary objective was to find an area out of the wind where they could hole up and huddle together until dawn. The thieving stranger hadn't taken the blanket Vicky found in Bob's cache, so at least they had the means to keep out some of the cold and their body heat in. They wrapped themselves in each other's arms and snuggled as closely as possible, but even then, were too cold to actually get any sleep, which wouldn't come anyway considering the anxiety they both felt about their new situation.

"We're never going to get to that reservation like this," Jonathan said. "You're going to have to go on without me tomorrow. There's no other option."

"Leaving you is *not* an option, Jonathan. Don't even go there."

"I'm serious, Vicky. You've got to be realistic. How far do you think I can limp on one leg and a crutch? And look how slow I am! I'll be lucky to make four or five miles a day, if I can even hold up to that."

"Four or five miles is still better than nothing. Even if it's only one mile a day, we'll find a way, Jonathan."

"No, because we don't have enough food for both of us to waste that much time out here. Not to mention there'll be another snowstorm coming soon, no doubt."

"We've got the revolver. I'll shoot the next animal we see. Maybe we can even get a deer. Then, we'll be set."

"That won't fix the problem of me being unable to hike out of here. It doesn't make sense for both of us to freeze to death out here, Vicky. If we do, there'll be no one to tell Eric what happened to Shauna."

"Eric will find my note. He may have already, for all we know. It's been long enough since he left, especially if he found Megan there at the reservation. Even if not, he'll be long gone by the time I could hike there. Without Tucker, I just don't see the point in focusing on that reservation. We need to think survival first and that means finding someplace more sheltered, at a much lower elevation if possible. After that maybe I can find another horse or someone we can trust to give us a ride if we can make it to a road. But in the meantime, I'm not leaving you Jonathan."

"You know you can't trust anybody you may meet on the roads, and who would give you another horse? You have no way to pay for it even if anyone would be willing to sell one. I guess you could steal one if you get lucky, but then we're no better than that son of a bitch that took Tucker."

"You're right, but I'm just thinking out loud. We'll find a way though, Jonathan, whatever it takes. But we're sticking together to do it."

Jonathan could see that there was no point in arguing this further at the moment. Vicky would realize soon enough that he was right and come to her senses. He would do his best to walk with her help and the crutch, and she would see that they were getting nowhere like that. But when they pulled the blanket around them to wait for dawn, Vicky snuggled closer to him than ever in the darkness, and then suddenly, he felt her warm lips against his and he forgot about the dire circumstance of their situation. What had seemed an impossible dream was coming true, and Jonathan never wanted that feeling to end. He no longer wanted Vicky to leave him behind either. In the morning, he would walk, no matter how much it hurt, and no matter where they were going as long as they were together.

"I knew you were a good guy before I even met you, Jonathan," Vicky said, when Jonathan told her he hadn't expected that to happen. "When Eric told me about you, I knew. You're strong and brave and you've been helping him and Shauna, and not just thinking about yourself. Is there anything more important in the world we live in now?"

She couldn't see him blushing in the dark but hearing her say that helped him understand a little. Maybe it was natural for women to gravitate to those things when they felt their world was falling apart and dangers were all around, but he still felt like Vicky was way out of his league. Would she even give him a second glance in any other circumstance? Jonathan doubted it, but feeling her body close to him, he decided it no longer mattered. Like Eric frequently said, *now* was all that mattered. You couldn't go back to the past and the future didn't yet exist. And if *now* was all that was real, then Jonathan figured it was a pretty great reality, despite the fact that he and Vicky no longer had a horse and he could barely walk. He didn't want the intensity of this *now* to end, but when morning came, both of them knew they had to keep moving if they were to survive. Getting to lower elevation was the first priority, and finding more food was next.

They finished off the last bits of meat from the bones of the rabbit they'd cooked the evening before, leaving the meager rations remaining from Bob's cache untouched to sustain them later. Vicky suggested that they stop every half hour to give Jonathan a five-minute break, and he didn't argue. He gave it all his effort while they were moving, and slowly but surely, they made their way downhill until the makeup of the forest changed from alpine spruce and fir to more open woods with pine and cedar the predominate species. They camped and shared one of the last two freeze-dried meals and left the next morning without eating at all. Another day of slow, but steady progress found them resting in a sunny spot on a west-facing slope when they took a long afternoon break, and naturally fell into each other's arms again before dozing off for a short nap to make up for lost sleep during the cold nights.

When Jonathan opened his eyes again, Vicky was crouching beside him, her hand over his mouth as she bent low and whispered. "Someone's coming, Jonathan! It's the man who stole Tucker! He's got him with him now!"

"What?" Jonathan lifted himself up to his elbows when Vicky removed her hand from his mouth. "Where?"

"Down there," she pointed, keeping her hand low and her movements slow and deliberate so the person she was referring to wouldn't see.

Jonathan could see him now. He was down in the mostly open meadow that they had just crossed earlier before they stopped here to rest. The man was walking slowly, and leading three horses, one of which was definitely Tucker!

"I think he's following us, Vicky! See how he's looking at the ground? That's exactly the way we came!"

"But why would he do that? He already took the horse and everything he wanted. We don't have much but the little bit of food he left and the revolver. Do you think he came back for that?"

Jonathan didn't think so, but looking at Vicky, he wondered if she might be the reason the man was back. Maybe he'd thought about it after he rode away into the night? Jonathan wondered now if he'd already had the other horses or if he'd somehow managed to steal them after taking Tucker. Regardless of when he got them, Vicky was right. The low-life bastard was a fucking horse thief! At the moment, he was still too far away for Jonathan to clearly see his face, and unfortunately, the scope he'd taken off of Shauna's ruined rifle was among the things the thief had taken. But from the way he was following their trail, Jonathan knew it wouldn't be long before they got a close up look at him without it.

"We've got to stay down and out of sight right here and ambush him, Vicky. It's our only chance. If we try to move now, he'll see us, and even if we get away, he'll find us if he was able to follow our trail this far."

"You want to ambush and shoot him? With the revolver?"

"Yes. It's all we *can* do. But we've got to wait until he gets in close, because if I miss, we'll be screwed. It looks like he's got more firepower than the .45-70 he took from us. That's an AK he's carrying now."

The wait seemed to take forever, as the man was moving slowly and deliberately, studying the ground here and there and stopping often to scan his surroundings. As he got closer, less than a hundred yards away, he stopped and stared straight in their direction each time he found more of their tracks, and Jonathan broke out into a cold sweat. Had the man already spotted them hiding there, and they just didn't know it? If he opened up on them with that rifle, they wouldn't have a chance. Jonathan knew he couldn't afford to wait. He slowly eased the revolver forward from where he was stretched out prone behind a rock. He steadied it with both hands, but the long barrel was still shaking, and he knew if he didn't control it, his first bullet would go wild, and with it the element of surprise that was their only chance. Vicky was right behind him, looking over his shoulder in silence as they waited.

"Just a little closer," Jonathan whispered, knowing he needed to let the man close half the distance between them before he had a solid chance of hitting him. He was coming, but it was taking forever. When the man came into their camp in the dark, it had been freezing cold and he was wearing a heavy coat with a hood pulled down over most of his head, and had his face covered with a bandana. He and Vicky hadn't been able to see anything of his features, but now his head and face were uncovered, and Jonathan could see that he had long raven-colored hair that hung past his shoulders. The stranger looked Native American or possibly Hispanic, but seeing his skill at tracking, Jonathan imagined the former was more likely, and the ease with which he carried the AK and handled the horses made him seem all the more dangerous. Jonathan knew he couldn't afford to mess this up. Everything rested on his ability to make that first shot. His finger was taking up the slack in the trigger when the man stopped and stared directly at him again, as if he could somehow see him hidden among the rocks up there. It was disconcerting enough to cause Jonathan to waste a precious second or two, and in those seconds the man dropped the leads of the horses and dove for cover before he could squeeze off a shot. When he *did* actually pull the trigger, Jonathan was shooting at nothing; his target had seemingly melted into the scant brush surrounding him. Jonathan fired two more rounds at the area where he'd seen him vanish and then stopped, realizing there were only three left in the cylinder and that he was facing an adversary armed with an AK-47 and a 30-round magazine.

Eighteen

UNTIL SHE WOKE FROM her nap and saw they were being followed, Vicky had been feeling pretty good about things that second afternoon because Jonathan was still able to make progress, despite that they were both tired and weak, and their food was running out. Before they stopped to rest on the hillside overlooking the meadow, they had already talked about camping nearby and trying to shoot another rabbit or whatever game animal they could find before moving on again the next day. When she woke from her nap, the first thing she thought of was that she should take the revolver and try her luck. They'd seen deer tracks down there in the meadow earlier, so when she sat up, she glanced that way to see if she could see anything moving. But what she saw shattered her illusions that they were somehow okay.

When the horse thief had left without harming them and had even gone so far as to leave their revolver behind, Vicky had assumed he might really be a good person at heart, despite what she'd said about him. She knew a lot of people were being driven to desperation by the present circumstances in this crazy new reality, and many of them were resorting to looting and robbery in order to survive. But seeing him there now, apparently tracking them down, changed everything. It made no sense for him to follow them here, especially at the slow pace they were traveling, when he seemed in such a hurry that night he robbed them. But whatever he'd told them about needing to get back to his family was obviously a lie. And besides, he had two more horses besides Tucker, but wasn't riding any of them because he was walking slowly instead, stopping to study the ground for their footprints. When she quietly woke Jonathan, the fear in her voice was impossible to hide.

Jonathan was as shocked as she was when he saw the man coming, and she knew he was right when he said they had to turn the tables on him and ambush him before he knew they were aware he was tracking them. With only one weapon between them though, all she could do was keep her fingers crossed and hope he wouldn't miss as Jonathan prepared to take the shot. But when their stalker seemed to see them at the last minute, right before Jonathan pulled the trigger, Vicky saw him drop to the ground and then it was almost as if the earth swallowed him up. She knew he was still there somewhere though, and she fully expected that she and Jonathan would be cut to pieces by incoming fire from his AK at any moment. Jonathan wanted her to run for it while she could, but there was no way Vicky was leaving him now.

Even if she could get away by doing so, she knew she wouldn't want to live, knowing he was killed because of her. She'd only known the guy such a short time that it probably didn't make sense to feel that way, but Vicky suspected she was falling in love whether she wanted to or not.

"Maybe you hit him after all," she whispered when the silence lingered on long minutes after the echoes of the .44 Magnum died away.

"No, I don't think so. I think he was completely out of my line of sight before I pulled the trigger."

"Maybe…" Vicky's next thought was cut short by a sudden shout from the direction where the man had vanished.

"If you're through shooting at me, perhaps we can talk?" It was him, but Vicky still couldn't see him out there among the grass and low bushes where he was hiding. "You are Jonathan and Vicky, is that right?" He continued.

How in the hell could he possibly know that? Vicky wondered. Jonathan looked back at her with the same question written on his face.

"I've been following your trail all the way from the cabin where you were staying. I came there with Eric Branson to get you two and his wife, Shauna!"

Vicky had heard enough to think that this was completely crazy, but she had to respond: "Then why did you sneak up on our camp the night before last and rob us? Why did you steal our stuff and my horse, Tucker?"

There was a long silence before the still-hidden man replied. "I didn't steal any horses, but I did run into a fellow riding yours. I knew when I saw it that it was the animal I was tracking by the gait, and by the description Eric gave me. That man claimed he found the horse wandering in the mountains, but I could tell he was lying by the look in his eyes. Now he is the one wandering, and with no horse and no guns!"

"I think he's for real, Vicky!" Jonathan said. "He wouldn't know about Eric if he wasn't!" Jonathan shouted back to the man: "If you're serious, then show yourself, but keep your hands where I can see them!"

The man suddenly stood, and when he did, he was much closer to them than Vicky would have thought. How he did that, she had no idea, but his hands were empty and out to his side, indicating he was putting all his faith in Jonathan.

"Take it easy kid! Eric told me you could get nervous sometimes, but I'm not here to hurt you! When we found your trail and then the burned cabin and your note, Eric and the others went on to look for Shauna. They sent me to track you down and take you back to the reservation. Megan and Aaron are already there; waiting."

"Megan and Aaron made it to the reservation?" Vicky had to hear it again.

"Yes, they are both there now. It will be easier to talk about all this if we sit down together and put away our guns. Eric Branson is my friend, so if you are friends of his, then you are friends of mine."

"Sure," Jonathan said. "I'm sorry I fired at you."

"You didn't know who I was, and I didn't see you until the last minute, although I had a bad feeling something wasn't right, like I was being watched. I didn't figure it out for sure until I saw a reflection on that stainless-steel revolver you were pointing at me. If not for that, I guess you'd have blown my head off!"

"Well, I'm glad I didn't make that mistake, man, I really am! But what I want to know is how you disappeared like that so fast! That was some crazy shit, dude!"

"Old Apache trick! Maybe I will teach you, someday. They call me Wolf, by the way."

"It's good to meet you, Wolf. I've never met an Apache Indian before! Dude, I'm sure glad me and Vicky aren't your enemies. We wouldn't have a chance, the way you tracked us down!"

"Following a trail is easy if you know what to look for. I could show you that too and you could do it pretty well with a little practice."

"But what about Shauna?" Vicky asked. "I'm surprised Eric didn't want you to try and track her instead? Or did Eric find my note and decide it was impossible because the men that took her drove away with her after they got her to their vehicles?"

"No, it's never impossible, and Eric did go after her. Our best tracker, Luke, is with him. If anyone can figure out where they went after they left that place, it is Luke."

Vicky had walked over to Tucker's side by this time and was whispering to him and telling him how happy she was to see him again, when she'd thought she never would.

"We can all ride now," Wolf said. "I brought the extra horse with me because I knew you only had one. But I guess it was just luck that I ran into that guy who stole yours. He was headed back in the direction from which you came." Wolf showed them the guns he'd taken from the man too; there were two of them, and Jonathan confirmed they were Bart's .45-70 and his .22 Magnum he had stashed in his cache. "I wish I'd had a chance to meet the old man," Wolf said when Vicky described the cache and Jonathan told him a couple of Bob's stories. "It sounds like he had the true spirit of the wilderness, a man at home in the mountains."

They were soon to find out that Wolf was quite at home out there too. He had a little food with him from what he'd packed when the group left the reservation, but since they found the cabin burned and the supplies gone, the restocking they'd planned on hadn't happened. But in addition to his AK-47 that he carried as his fighting weapon, Wolf had his trusty Winchester .30-.30, and with that he went out hunting after they decided to stay where they were for the night. When he returned, he had a small doe lashed behind his saddle. "It's cold enough that most of the meat won't spoil, so I figured it wouldn't hurt to take a deer, even if it's more than we can eat on this journey. You never know what delays we may run into, but even if there are none, it's still a long ride back to the reservation.

That night Vicky sat close to Jonathan on one side of the fire as Wolf sat opposite, answering their questions about the Jicarilla and the reservation and telling them about growing up there and then joining the Marines with several of his buddies, some of whom were with Eric now. Wolf was honest with them and said that despite what he'd said earlier about how it was never impossible to follow a trail, things didn't look good for Shauna. This wasn't anything Vicky and Jonathan didn't already know, but Wolf assured them that his Apache friends that accompanied Eric would stick with him, and not give up the search until he made that decision for himself. He told them what he knew of the cartels that were operating in the area, and how he expected it was only going to get worse unless something was done quickly to discourage the incursions. He said that Nantan and the others on the security force were ready and willing to do so, but there were only so many of them, and that even though they'd gone with Eric to learn what they could of the situation, they would avoid unnecessary confrontations that far from home, as protecting their people there was the top priority.

Vicky could tell that Jonathan was fascinated with Wolf the way Shauna had said he was with Bob Barham. Jonathan had never met anyone remotely like either of them growing up in south Florida, but he was an outdoorsman at heart and could really look up to men such as these that had skills and knowledge far beyond his own. Wolf's arrival meant their immediate worries about survival could be put aside. The man had complete confidence that he could get them safely to the reservation, and Vicky fully trusted him already. She knew she would sleep well that night, although with Wolf nearby, she and Jonathan would have to be more discreet about their newfound intimacy. She wasn't bothered by that at all though, as she felt that her time of getting to know him was just beginning. Whatever the future held for them, she hoped they would be together, even if it meant following him to Louisiana. Whether he would go there or not was dependent upon what happened with Eric. Jonathan said that if Eric didn't find Shauna soon, he had no idea what it might mean for his plans to take Megan back to the boat he had waiting there.

"I think he'll eventually go," Jonathan said, when Vicky brought it up as they lay there whispering after Wolf fell asleep. "I mean, Megan's the reason he came back, not

Shauna. I know he'll do everything he can to try and find her, but if he can't, Megan will be his priority."

"There's no way she's going to agree to go though, and leave her mom missing out here. I know her pretty well. I can't see her doing it. And, we don't exactly know what's up with her and Aaron either. I mean, she left with him when she broke up with Gareth. They may be pretty tight by now, you never know. If they are, she's not gonna want to leave him here. And since he's pretty into his heritage and tribal stuff and all that, he may not be willing to leave that behind to go off sailing across the ocean."

"Yeah, I can see that. It's kind of gotten complicated for Eric. His whole plan in the beginning was so simple. He told me all about it, how he thought he would just sneak right in to the coast in his kayak and find Megan and her mom there at their house on a nearby canal. But of course, they were gone because of the hurricane, and then he met me and that was the beginning of his complications, taking me with him."

"I don't imagine he saw it that way. Look how much you've helped him since."

"Maybe, but I know I was a pain in his ass in the beginning. And then when we finally got to his dad's place and found Shauna there, her new husband was the next problem. *He* was an even bigger pain in the ass and complication!"

"From the way I saw her looking at Eric just the few days I was around them, I don't think she's thinking about her husband much. She sure didn't talk about him to me."

"Probably because she never really wanted to divorce Eric in the first place. I think she tried and tried to make it work with him, and finally gave up. It literally took a war back here at home to get his attention, but I know he regrets the way he neglected his family before. He told me that several times. He's probably really feeling like shit about now, with Shauna missing after the way he left us all in that cabin. He's blaming himself, and he's super pissed at those guys that came there and took her. I almost feel sorry for any of those poor bastards he finds. He's going to take it all out on them. He really is!"

* * *

By the time Eric, Shauna and Luke hiked back to the road and then rode with Nantan and the others back to the work station compound where they'd left the horses, it was nearly midnight. The chief didn't really kill his man, Wilson, like he said he was going to do, but the two of them didn't seem to be on speaking terms when Eric and Nantan unlocked the supply room and led them out.

"You'll find out why he talked soon enough," Nantan told him, "because you will do the same when it is your turn."

They had already made up their minds to take the chief back to the reservation with them; first so that Nantan and the security council could interrogate him about all the operations he might know of in the region that affected Jicarilla land. And after they were done with him, Eric figured he could leverage delivering him to the Army for his crimes in exchange for help with the transportation problem he was facing in getting his family to Louisiana. That would all come later though, of course. At the moment, Eric was under pressure from Shauna to get back to that reservation ASAP so that she could see with her own eyes that Megan was there and safe.

"There's plenty of fuel here in the storage tanks," Tommy assured him when Eric questioned the feasibility of just driving there. Returning by horseback was the safest and surest bet, but it would take much longer and since they didn't have a specific reason to go back through the high country in the vicinity of the cabin, there was no point in subjecting Shauna to such a journey after all she'd recently been through. Nantan and the others agreed. They had enough firepower to fight their way out of most situations they might encounter, and the chief and Wilson would be additional insurance.

"They will both understand what will happen to them if they steer us into a C.R.I. checkpoint or some other trap. I will make the consequences very clear to them, and Wilson is already a believer!" Nantan said.

Luke and Tommy volunteered to take the long way back, riding the horses, so with that decided, Eric wanted to go ahead and roll out that very night, saying it was riskier to stay there at the compound than to be on the road, considering how they could be trapped there at the end of a dead-end.

"We'll take the two best trucks and all of the weapons and ammo we can find here, in addition to what we already have. I'll drive one of them and Shauna will ride shotgun with me. Nantan, you or Red can drive the other. We'll secure the prisoners and put them in the back of yours, and I'll follow behind."

Shauna, of course, was delighted with this arrangement, as she wanted nothing more to do with that compound and had no interest in staying put anywhere until she saw Megan. Another night without sleep would make little difference now, and she was so wired and excited about the prospect of seeing her daughter that she told Eric she would be wide awake that night anyway as they got into the truck to leave.

"I'll be happy to drive if you like. I'm really not tired, Eric."

"No, I've got it. Try and get some sleep on the way. I'll wake you if I need you or if we run into trouble, but I don't expect we will. Nantan worked out the shortest route that avoids highways, and he said that with the roads empty like they are now, we'll be there by midmorning if we don't stop. You'll be glad you slept when we arrive, because you and Megan are going to have a lot to talk about!"

"We *all* have a lot to talk about, Eric. This is just so surreal, I can't believe that it's happening!"

About the Author

SCOTT B. WILLIAMS HAS been writing about his adventures for more than twenty-five years. His published work includes dozens of magazine articles and twenty-five books, with more projects currently underway. His interest in backpacking, sea kayaking and sailing small boats to remote places led him to pursue the wilderness survival skills that he has written about in his popular survival nonfiction books and travel narratives such as *On Island Time: Kayaking the Caribbean*, an account of a two-year solo kayaking expedition he undertook at age 25. With the release of *The Pulse: A Novel of Surviving the Collapse of the Grid* in 2012, Scott moved into writing fiction full time. His post-apocalyptic and action & adventure stories draw heavily on his personal wilderness and ocean experiences to create believable scenarios often set in dire circumstances. To learn more about his upcoming books or to contact Scott, visit his website: www.scottbwilliams.com

Made in the USA
San Bernardino, CA
07 December 2019